I0450932

Dared to Bare

Lucy Lafferty

Published by Lynda French, 2024.

This is a work of fiction. Similarities to real people, places, or events are entirely coincidental.

DARED TO BARE

First edition. March 10, 2024.

ISBN: 978-1998074259

Written by Lucy Lafferty.

To those who enjoy administering or receiving a *"good girl spanking"*... have fun with this!

Dared to Bare

Derek knows I want to talk to him about something, he keeps giving me his *friendly and inquisitive* look that invites me to open up. But I can't, not tonight.

He's fourteen years older than me and while that's normally not an issue sometimes well... sometimes it is.

It's all Cathy's fault. She's my work buddy and she kind of pushed me into agreeing to something that was funny at the time but now? Not so much. Derek might not approve. But a dare is a dare!

I work in the head office of a company that makes tires and our jobs are all clerical so almost all the staff are women. *Departments* is a grand word for our different sections since some, like mine, only have three people. But our lunch schedule is based on department so Cathy and Shelby and I share the staff-room with the Data Entry girls who are a young, rowdy bunch.

It's impossible not to overhear their conversations and today's talk was especially raucous. Their supervisor even had to come in to tell them to keep it down, the whole floor could hear their loud laughter.

Apparently one of their crew is getting married so they had a bridal shower for fun sexual gifts like dildos, massage oils, edible panties, that sort of thing. And they got talking about the entertainment they had which was watching that *Fifty Shades of Grey* movie on DVD.

Long story short, Cathy dared me to ask Derek if he'd ever thought about us trying spanking as foreplay, and if he would want to, and she promised she'd ask Guy, her husband, the same thing. Shelby's off the hook because she's single and not dating anyone right now.

So I agreed, but now I can't bring myself to say anything to Derek. Cathy's going to laugh her head off at me tomorrow for being such a chicken and backing down from the dare.

I could pretend I did ask and tell her Derek said *No, not interested...* but I'm lousy at lying. She'll figure it out and that'll just make her laugh at me even more. She and Shelby love teasing me about still being a newlywed.

When we settle into bed and kiss goodnight Derek asks: "Was there something you wanted to talk about? Or tell me, Polly?"

But I just say *No Hon, nothing* and turn my lying face away from him.

I'm dragging my butt this morning because I had a sleepless night tossing and turning while trying to figure out what to say to Cathy. She's such a strong woman.

I'll bet she said to Guy something like: *Hey, this is a hoot – have you ever wanted to give me a spanking? Just like in that Fifty Shades movie? The girls at work want to know!*

Maybe I could say it like that to Derek? I realize I have to say something, it's almost eight-thirty and I have to leave for the office so I'm running out of time. There's no way I can face Cathy if I don't ask.

"Derek hon, um... at work yesterday? Uh, the girls from Data Entry were all talking about... um, have you heard of that movie Fifty Shades of Grey? I think it was a book, actually. Do you know it?"

"Polly, whatever you're trying to say just say it. It was obvious all night that you have something on your mind."

"OK, you're right. It's just well... it's a stupid dare. Cathy said she and I both had to ask our husbands if they'd ever wanted to spank us, like in that movie? You know, as a sex thing. So, um, have you?"

"Have I heard of that movie? Yes. But, I'm not quite clear about what you're saying. Polly, are you asking me to spank you?"

"No! Well, I guess... er, I'm asking if you ever *thought* about doing it."

"Swatting a luscious ass like yours? Of course I have!"

Suddenly Derek has moved right up against me and is holding me close. I'm very aware of his muscular chest, his musky manly smell, his strong arms...

My temperature has soared and my voice sounds breathless when I squeak out: "Oh!"

Derek pushes the hair out of my eyes so I can't avoid his penetrating gaze and he smiles, asking: "I guess since yesterday's conversation with Cathy you've been thinking about me spanking you, hmm? So, is that something you'd like us to explore, baby girl?"

I always get shivers when he calls me baby girl.

"Um, well I... I guess we could, uh, well if..."

Fortunately he rescues me from my inarticulate babbling with a kiss. A deep strong kiss. I melt into it and his smile widens when he says: "I think I've got my answer."

I just stare up at him, obviously I'm incapable of coherent speech this morning.

"It's just too bad you didn't say something last night, Polly. Otherwise we could have really given you something to talk about with your coworkers. Although I'm not sure if I like the idea of you gossiping about our private lives—"

"Oh no, I don't! I mean, we kid around. If I'm in a good mood Cathy or Shelby will say *somebody got lucky last night!* and I usually answer by just waving them off or I say *are you jealous?* But that's it. I never get specific. They wouldn't expect me to and vice versa. That would be embarrassing."

"I'm glad to hear that because what happens between us is very special to me and it's not something I want to share."

"It's special to me too, Derek. You know I love you."

"I know, Polly. And you have my permission to tell Cathy and Shelby that I'm looking forward to putting you across my knee – someday."

"Oh! Really?"

"Definitely! Now hurry up, you're going to be late."

It felt good to let the girls know I hadn't chickened out after all.

Cathy told us that Guy said: *Sure thing sweetie, anytime you want to drop your drawers and bend over I'll be happy to smack your ass.* They've been married for eighteen years and she says she hasn't had the urge yet so it's pretty unlikely that anything like that will ever happen.

"Maybe if you watched the movie you'd be interested?" commented Shelby.

"You just want me to rent it and then lend it to you so you don't have to be the one all embarrassed at the video store."

"Ha-ha you're wrong, I've already seen it. I saw it in the theater on the big screen."

That got my attention and I asked Shelby to tell us about it.

"Well really it's a love story. I mean sure there's this whole discipline thing and signing a contract but overall it's romance. He does put her over his knee but when he sees that she seems to like the spanking he stops. In a later scene though he hits her with a belt and that part was icky."

"Were you on a date when you saw the movie?"

"No! But I wish I had of been. But only if it had been with a hot guy I was involved with, right? I mean it sure as hell wouldn't have been a good idea for a first date!"

We all laugh at that then Cathy asks: "So what exactly did Derek say, Polly?"

"He said something about my butt being luscious so he'd probably like to spank me someday."

"Oooh, sounds like you just need to provoke him and he'll punish you."

"I don't want to be punished! I mean, if we did do something like that it would just be foreplay, right? Not some anger thing or some weird kinky thing. Just for fun."

"Well, when it does happen you know you'll have to tell us all about it."

"Well, you know I'll do no such thing!"

We all laughed when Cathy cried: "Spoilsport!"

Derek works from home so, as usual, he was already waiting with glasses of wine poured when I got in. I kicked off my shoes and joined him on the couch saying *Cheers* and then, after taking a drink *Ahhhh*.

I love this ritual of having a drink and ten or fifteen minutes of relaxing while discussing each other's news. I often leave a casserole out to thaw and Derek will pop it in a low temperature oven so that dinner is waiting for whenever we're ready to eat.

Tonight I curl up on the sofa and Derek pulls my legs up onto his lap so he can give my feet a massage. It feels so good. I sigh with pleasure and proudly tell him that I'd *certainly held my own* against Cathy today.

"And did you spend any time fantasizing about having your panties taken down and your bottom bared for a good old-fashioned spanking?" he asked.

I can feel my eyes widen and suspect my pupils have dilated with excitement just like his have. I know Derek has noticed my interest and that makes me feel shy so I don't say anything.

"Because I found my thoughts drawn to this morning's chat again and again. In fact, I found it difficult to concentrate on my work. Eventually I finished, and then spent some time surfing the Internet. I found a lot of blogs, websites, even chatrooms – although they're private - all devoted to wife spanking."

I'm still tongue-tied.

"Some of it, well frankly most of it, didn't appeal to me. It was punishment, not play, and I would only be interested in spanking you for sexual pleasure. Of course any kind of spanking, by the very nature of the act, would involve some pain. The smacks must sting, and it must be sore when the skin turns red."

I nod to show I'm listening which is totally unnecessary because I'm hanging on his every word.

"What surprised me was the number of wives who apparently enjoyed the feeling of release – especially if they were *spanked to tears* – in the aftermath. Now, when it's a punishment spanking there is no sex, it's simply an act of discipline or correction. But still, most of the women remarked on how aroused they got. Even though the punishment spankings are quite severe using belts or paddles or other implements.

But I was just interested in spanking for sexual pleasure. Husbands hand spanking their wives is definitely a thing. But so is wives spanking husbands, bosses spanking staff – either person being male or female, mothers or fathers spanking sons and daughters... the vast majority of stories and books seem to be about using spanking to punish."

We sit in silence for a few minutes but it isn't particularly comfortable. There's so much unspoken conversation going on between us. Derek moves my feet to the floor and says that it's time to eat.

As we head into the kitchen he suggests that tomorrow I should wear a dress or skirt with a thong and no hosiery.

"Spend the day being aware of your bare flesh, feel the cool air, enjoy the sensation of the unfamiliar fabric of your dress rubbing your skin, focus on the sexiness of near nudity, and, since it's Friday, think about the hours and hours we'll have to enjoy our private playtime when you get home."

I discover that I'm very hungry and I eat a good dinner. I feel turned on but I'm awfully tired after last night's poor sleep so I go up to bed yawning.

Friday's are always easy since everyone's in a good mood about the weekend. A lot of the staff treat themselves to lunch out on a Friday, especially pay-day Friday.

This particular Friday is especially fun for me because I have done what Derek suggested. Of course his suggestions always sound more like orders... he does have a very strong, dominant personality, but I like it.

So, I've enjoyed hugging the secret to myself that I'm practically naked, well, actually I am naked under my skirt. My thong leaves me with only the teeniest bit of fabric wrapped round my privates.

Thoughts of what awaits me – *possibly* awaits me - tonight have occupied my mind and left me excited and anxious. I've experienced a number of new and interesting sensations and discovered when I visited the ladies room that I'm moist and aroused.

I'm afraid I'm a bit of a prude about sexual matters, or maybe not so much prudish as just ignorant in my knowledge of them, so not being covered up is unusual and freeing. I feel quite daring. Actually, I feel quite slutty.

No! I feel *naughty* and slutty. I wonder what Cathy and Shelby would say if they knew!

Now I understand that Derek *wants* me to feel this way. He wants me to be the saucy, slutty, naughty wife who needs to feel the strength of her man's firm hand teaching her a lesson. God, just thinking that phrase has me quivering. I know it's just a game we're playing but still.. great foreplay technique!

I'm feeling both anticipation and apprehension on the way home. My mind wanders until a blast from someone's car horn - when I linger too long after the light turns green - brings me back down to earth. For the rest of the trip I'm careful to concentrate on my driving.

As soon as I open the front door and smell pizza I'm delighted. First, it's a great idea; secondly, it's a treat we don't have very often since I'm supposed to be watching my weight; and finally, it doesn't have to be eaten right away. Not if we're... delayed.

We greet each other with a kiss and when Derek hands me a glass of wine I gulp it down. He raises an eyebrow but doesn't say anything, simply pours me another.

Okay, I admit it, I'm a bit nervous about what's to come.

But apparently nothing is coming because he suggests we eat the pizza while it's still piping hot.

"Cold pizza is great for breakfast but dinner pizza has to be hot!" he declares.

I quickly set the table and put out the food. He's also bought garlic bread which won't be a problem breath-wise since we'll both be eating it. The pizza, the bread, and the wine all taste wonderful.

"Let's skip coffee," Derek says, "and just enjoy the buzz from the wine. In fact, I'll open another bottle."

He leaves the room to do that and I stack up our plates and carry everything over to the counter. I just emptied the dishwasher this morning and want to run a cleaning cycle. I don't want to load it again and since there's very little washing up I fill the sink with hot water and get started by hand.

Coming back with the bottle Derek tops up my glass and clinks it with his. He leans back against the counter, half-turned to he can face me. I feel his eyes travel over my body as he says:

"You've been teasing me with a hint of cleavage all through dinner. I want to see more."

The top I have on has a lower-than-usual neckline, I can only wear it with a low-cut bra. I noticed his eyes on me and have to confess I've been posing and preening to catch his eye since I walked through the front door.

Putting his wineglass down he reaches over to pull the scoop-necked t-shirt over my head. A few suds from the dishwater fly up and settle in my hair.

This bra I'm wearing is quite a flimsy affair that doesn't really provide me with the support I need, and it's so skimpy my breasts overflow. However it is the matching piece to my thong.

Derek enjoys a long look at my mostly exposed breasts and smiles at the sight of my nipples growing hard and dark under his gaze.

Moving behind me he unzips my skirt and lets it drop, holding it open so I can easily step out. Now he'll see that I did follow his instructions about wearing next-to-nothing to work today.

The view he has of the back of me is almost entirely bare. I feel self-conscious, aware that I'm at least fifteen pounds overweight. Sure, he's vocal in his admiration of my *pleasingly plump derriere* but can he also see the roll of fat over my bra strap? Or the extra swell over my hip?

When we're in bed I know he can feel my overweight body, especially my squishy belly, but I also know that my skin is very soft and smooth and I warm him up nicely. However, I don't like having him look at me like this, especially under the harsh kitchen light, and I feel uncomfortable.

With a couple of fingers he traces lines right across both bare cheeks and I feel my flesh goosepimpling at his touch. I stand frozen in place up to my elbows in hot, soapy water while my husband ogles my near-naked body. A body that I think is far too fat.

Pressing up against me he gestures that I should finish the dishes while he strokes and caresses my arms and breasts. When he speaks his voice is low and oh so sexy.

"After all the reading and web-surfing that I've done I could draw a blueprint on how to punish your wife's bottom but there's surprisingly little to read about pleasure spankings.

"Wh-what's the difference?" I ask in a timid voice.

"Oh punishment truly is punishment, and it's brutal. It usually begins with a hard hand-spanking of many, many swats until the hmm, what shall we call her? victim? offender? let's stick with wife. He spanks until the wife's flesh is very sore and red. Then the husband moves on to the second spanking."

"But why? I mean, if she's already red—"

"Because the punishment has to be shameful – so he'll make her stand in a corner to think about why she's being spanked – as well as being painfu. The wife must be spanked until she's sobbing. That's how the man knows she's learned her lesson."

"So the second spanking is..."

"It's done with some sort of implement. I think the most common method is for the man to take off his belt, double it up, and start laying down stripes. For that he's probably got her bent over the sofa or the end of the bed so he can really swing his arm. He's careful to keep the buckle covered up in his hand because he doesn't want to cut or unnecessarily bruise her body. The rump can take a great deal of punishing smacks but cuts and bruises need time to heal.

Then the wife is sent to stand in the corner again to reflect on what she's done and why she's been punished. If the husband is satisfied she's taken her correction as intended then all is forgiven and she continues with a clean slate. That is the point where the women who enjoy being subservient wives feel comfort. But if she is unrepentant or angry well..."

"Well what?" I whisper.

He continues massaging and caressing my breasts as he explains: "Then he spanks her again but with something else. Probably another hard hand-spanking first, followed up with the paddle this time. He paddles her burning bottom until she promises never to defy him again.

Once she acknowledges that he's done the right thing by punishing her severely then he knows the discipline has been effective, and he can now comfort his penitent wife."

"Oh... um, Derek?"

"Don't worry Polly, we're not considering that kind of spanking, not ever. No, we're spanking for fun, for pleasure, just foreplay. But, as I mentioned, there's very little written about our type of spanking. The punishment kind is far more... popular.

In fact, I only read two things about pleasure spanking: the recommendation that it should always be administered by hand to easily distinguish which type of spanking the husband is giving, and also so he can feel the heat building up on his palm and know how hot his wife is feeling it."

I can't even managed an *Oh* this time, I can only gulp.

"Also, punishment spanking is usually non-sexual while pleasure spanking ends with great sex."

He leans over me to pull out the plugs from the two sinks and while we watch both the sudsy and the clear waters drain away tells me it's time to head upstairs.

"I'll finish here and will join you shortly. Take your wine with you, Polly."

Last night was quite an extraordinary experience. My body went through a whole gamut of sensations, and emotionally I zigzagged from one extremity to the other.

Climbing the stairs I was so aware of how the thong panties exposed my wobbly bottom and was embarrassed. Really, I'm too young to have let myself go like this. As soon as I got in the bedroom I closed the curtains and left the table lamps off so the room would stay dim.

Then, I didn't know what to do with myself while I waited. I picked up my hairbrush to tidy up my blonde curls but got distracted by its smooth wooden oval backing. *That would work as a paddle, although a smaller sized one,* I think, *but why? Why am I thinking this? I don't want to be paddled, implements are for punishment spankings and they're meant to really hurt.*

I don't *think* I want to be hurt but... if that's the pathway to losing control then maybe it would be okay?

I mean, if I don't have the control then I don't have the responsibility. Not being held to account means it doesn't matter how naughty – how downright bad and slutty and dirty – I am. I think I would like that kind of freedom.

Derek is my lawful husband, after all, so it's not like I'm whoring around or anything. I will always be safe with him.

14

Derek doesn't keep me waiting long. I suspect he's just as keen to begin as I am but he lounges in the doorway just looking manly, tough, and dangerous. He gives me a lazy smile that sends the butterflies in my stomach into a tizzy. But it's the sparkle in his eyes, revealing his hungry excitement, that's got the butterflies moving down into my pussy.

Our bed is a four-poster with headboard and footboard so he has to sit on the side. Holding out his hand to me I reluctantly let myself be pulled forward.

"I just want you to sit on my lap," he reassures me, but once I'm settled he adds, "to begin with."

I struggle to hold in my tummy but that's hard to do sitting like this. Then he tells me to unhook my bra and *show him what I've got*. The words and his tone of voice make me hot.

It's a front closure so I undo the clasp and slowly pull it wide open, letting my breasts bounce free. He takes the bra from my hand and holding my two wrists together wraps the stretchy material around and around and around, tucking the ends in. I could get free if I struggle enough, but with my arms in this position my breasts, my best feature, are pushed up and out and look fabulous.

I can tell by the intense look in Derek's eyes and quickened breathing that he agrees.

He fondles me gently at first but his caresses soon turn to the rough kneading I like and his fingers open and close over my bountiful flesh. He pinches and flicks my nipples until they're swollen and I'm squirming. After giving me a hard, deep kiss he flips me face down across his knee.

With my arms stretched out in front of me my breasts hang free, and with my hands bound I can't protect myself, he can handle me however he likes. I trust Derek implicitly but knowing the power he has over me in this moment is a real turn-on.

He plays with my nipples some more, rubbing the palm of his left hand across both, while his right hand rubs circles over my bottom. The thong hides nothing, offering no coverage whatsoever, but he still pulls it down. Leaving it around my knees makes me feel more naked – *if that's even possible!*

Derek's fingers toying with my nipples is sending shivers right through me. I feel myself trembling with anticipation of what's to come. My skin has tightened with goosebumps and the muscles in my backside are clenching.

Now that I'm fully nude while bound I'm so aware of how exposed, helpless, and vulnerable I am. I'm utterly at the mercy of this man, my husband who vowed to love and cherish me, but... will consenting to a spanking in this submissive position awaken something darker in him? If so, is that what I want? and am secretly hoping?

The fingers of his right hand continue tracing a light pattern over my skin making all my nerve endings tingle and a moan escapes my lips. He enjoys making me wait, knowing how antsy I get.

"You look scrumptious Polly, and I'm going to wreck your adorable ass. Too bad you didn't leave the curtains open, or a light on, because now, since I won't be able to see how red you're getting, I'll just have to keep spanking and spanking and spanking until I think you're done."

His words drive me even deeper into a wanting, lustful, hunger. I'm shocked to feel my hips rising as I offer my bare flesh to him, inviting him to do a thorough job. It's an eye-opener to discover how much I want this spanking from this man, my older and dominant husband.

And then he began. I'm trying to recall exactly how I felt in the moment. I know it hurt – each spank really stings – and that made me flinch. My flinching, squealing, and crying out shamed and humiliated me but... the humiliation is exquisite because I'm putting on a show for my man.

An embarrassing show because he teased me about how my plump behind wobbled with each stroke, and how he'll think of this moment every time he eats a dessert of jiggly red jello. I'm mortified, but reassured when he tells me how much he's enjoying this performance from his fat-bottomed girl.

Derek is orchestrating my movements and I want to be his debased and degraded entertainment. I want my involuntary writhing and squirming to amuse him. I'm so wet I fear I'm dripping and each swat sends me rubbing as hard as I can against his cock which is thickening in response.

I can feel the heat spreading over both cheeks as he works hard to cover every inch.

The spanking does seem to go on forever and he's saying the most delicious things – phrases that trigger a lusty response from me - phrases like: *need to give this brat a good hard bare-bottomed spanking,* and *teach this sassy little girl a lesson she won't soon forget,* and *this naughty girl has earned a red-hot ass.* My ass sure did get hot and stayed that way for a long time, too!

Tears are streaming down my face but I'm not even aware I'm crying. I do remember kicking my legs and swivelling my hips frantically – futilely - trying to avoid his relentless, heavy hand. But mostly I just remember the heat that started in my bum but flooded right through my entire groin. My posturing over the rough denim of his jeans rubbed my clit raw until it got fully engorged and swollen and wet.

I feel disconnected from the loud smacking sound made with each impact. It seems impossible that this noise comes from my husband administering painful spanks that I've submitted willingly to. The sound, the sting, and the non-stop smack-smack-smack sensation, along with the aching arousal I feel, combine into sensory overload. I finally stop fighting and just wilt, weeping.

When the spanking stopped the room was so quiet. All I could hear was his heavy breathing and my gasping, sobbing breaths. Then he started stroking my pussy from top to bottom and the wet sucking sound I make is so shamefully loud. My face burns red to match my sore inflamed bottom.

I can't prevent a groan escaping my lips but I don't know if it's one of dismay or arousal.

"Such a good girl! You took that really well and I'm very pleased with you, Polly. You're my very good little girl."

My heart sings to hear him compliment and praise me. Obviously he's really enjoyed spanking me and I'm proud I could take everything he gave. I don't care if my poor ass is burning, it's worth it to get this approval from him.

He only needs to turn halfway round to push me onto all fours on the bed while he quickly undresses enough to fuck me doggie-style. I'm so wet he easily enters me in one hard stroke, driving his long cock in to the hilt then steadily slides back and forth, pounding me roughly.

A couple of times a week Derek and I make love in a pleasant and pleasing manner but last night we fucked, we screwed, he nailed me, he hammered me. It was so erotically, excitingly, intensely *Hot! Hot! Hot!*

He kept saying he loved me, and loved fucking me, and how my very wet pussy proved I loved being spanked hard by him, and how it feels so fantastic to fuck me when I'm all slippery like this. I can't recall everything he was saying but I definitely remember how happy his words made me feel. Even when he said wouldn't let me cum until I agreed that I'd loved every minute across his knee.

He was holding my hips as he pounded into me and described how hot my flesh felt pressed against him and that he'd paddled my ass to a beautiful shade of red. He asked me if it was sore and when I answered *I'm very sore* he smugly replied *Good!*

I felt myself reaching a crescendo of passion and begged him to give me release.

"Admit you loved being spanked by me and then I'll give you permission to cum," he demanded.

"Yes! Yes! You can spank me whenever you want, Derek. I love it," I cried, writhing with the frustration of unfulfilled desire.

"And I love my fat-bottomed girl, so cum for me baby, I want to feel you all over my cock."

That orgasm was unlike any I'd ever had before. It felt like my soul took flight. I know that's a fanciful way to think but it was such a deep-rooted ecstasy drawn from the very core of my being.

Afterwards he took me into the bathroom where the light is bright and the full-length mirror enabled us both to see my blisteringly red-hot bottom. That sight turned us on all over again and while Derek sat on the chair I straddled him for another fucking.

He grabbed hold of my wrists, still bound by my bra, and pulled my arms straight up over my head. While my hips pogoed up and down on his cock my breasts bounced in his face and his grin was huge. I can only imagine what my expression looked like.

He grabbed my chin and turned me to look back over my shoulder growling at me with pride: "Look how I marked you, and that was just with my hand."

While I orgasmed again he grabbed and lifted my hips to rapidly slide me up and down the length of his shaft. As he pounded me my bottom burned against his thighs. Half-a-dozen hard thrusts sent me over the edge again and he joined me, calling out sharply.

We panted, spent, in each other's arms. Feeling our mingled cum dripping thickly over our legs. When I stood and staggered into the shower he was right behind me, steadying me. I'd lost track of how many times I orgasmed.

We soaped each other clean, then he gently toweled me dry before leading me back to the bedroom for a soothing session of him smoothing lotion into my tender skin. He said *this is called aftercare* and his online reading stressed the importance of this step.

It's not just to apply topical relief, its purpose includes intensifying the intimacy of our experience and attachment to one another.

He lightly massaged the lotion into my skin while applying a multitude of kisses *to make it all better.*

We both fell into deep, deep sleeps and I didn't waken until sunlight streamed into my eyes. Derek had just gotten up and he'd opened the curtains to examine my bottom in daylight.

He gently patted me, asking how I felt.

"A bit sore but not in a bad way, more like a well-used way."

That made him smile and he told me he definitely wanted me across his knee again but would wait until tonight to give me a chance to heal.

I pulled him back down on the bed and kneeling between his thighs began to lick and kiss and suck his balls until his dick grew hard. This was the first time I had ever initiated anything sexual between us, and the first time I took his dick in my mouth without being asked.

I slipped the head in and pulled him deeper and deeper gagging only when he reached the back of my throat but I managed to keep going. Using my tongue to swirl the tip I sucked hard so the insides of my cheeks wrapped him in wet warmth. His groans of pleasure were music to my ears.

After several minutes of me working my lips, tongue, and cheeks he lifted me up and onto his cock. While I rode him he used one hand to fondle my breasts and the other to tease my clit. Our bodies exploded in simultaneous orgasm - the best way to start the day - and with cold pizza to follow, too!

Saturday is chores day for both of us with Derek doing basement, yard, and garage work while I dust, polish, vacuum, and do the laundry. It seems strange to revert back to our usual patterns but the playtime of bed is separate from the routine of real life.

By early afternoon we were both ready for lunch, but when I bent down to get a saucepan for soup out of the drawer under the stove Derek was right there with his hands on my ass.

"I can't wait until tonight," he said in a tone of voice I'd never heard from him before.

Suddenly I'm bent over the kitchen table with him tugging my sweatpants and undies down and his hand smacking my exposed bottom.

This spanking is different. Being held across his knee is more intimate. I can feel the warmth of his body as it traps me, and I can feel his cock stirring beneath my pelvis. Being laid out like this is more clinical, more detached, more punishing... but equally arousing. I grip the edge of the table and feel my breasts crushing into the wooden surface with every swat.

In the broad light of day, in my domain – my kitchen – I'm being disciplined by my husband's firm hand.

I wish I could witness this spectacle that he's seeing. Instead, I have to imagine what an inviting sight his hand-prints make on my flesh. It's not fair that I can't look too!

All of sudden I'm inspired by an idea and call out to him to video us. It only takes a moment for him to grab his phone, position the camera, and get back to the spanking with renewed enthusiasm while creating a video to share with me. To shame me with because of how much it excites me.

I don't have to act in order to perform enticingly for the camera, I'm squirming and squealing like mad! Although my poor bottom is still red and sore from last night he doesn't hold back in giving me all he's got.

He spanks me all over announcing he's turned me a uniform shade of crimson red. Then he opines that he can deepen the color and does so with a flurry of quick sharp smacks. I'm on fire inside and out!

The thorough job he's doing ensures the happy result of a well-spanked wife, which translates into uninhibited joyful sex. I'll never look at my kitchen table in the same way again!

Derek discovered a real fondness for pleasure spanking and I felt his hand on my painful behind the whole weekend. I found myself across his knee, across the bed, across the back of the sofa, and even another stint over the kitchen table.

It's hard to find the right words to describe what I felt. I mean, it hurt, no question about that. A hard hand smacking a tender bottom is always going to be painful but what was happening to my ass was causing something new and exciting to happen everywhere else in my body and in my head, too.

I was so aroused, so horny, and I felt like such a naughty slut who needed the punishment my man was delivering. That's not my usual kind of thinking but something about being dominated and losing control, giving him all this power over me and my actions was so, so stimulating.

I started playacting so when he grabs my hand to yank me across his knee I immediately begin apologizing for being a brat and beg not to be spanked. He insists I've been *asking for it*. I wiggle provocatively, struggle as he pulls down my panties, and we both have great fun while I plead for mercy and he shows me none!

I'm sure his arm was tired by time he finished my session on Sunday night and it was the most painful - but also the most arousing of all - because he really caught me by surprise.

After repeated trips to our bed I needed another shower and was just finishing up when I heard Derek enter the bathroom. Our bathtub/ shower combo is roomy enough for two so I thought he was going to join me but when he didn't I turned off the water and poked my head around the curtain to grab my towel and see what he wanted.

"No drying off, not yet," he said, looking very serious. Reaching over he pulled the shower curtain right across revealing my naked wet body under the harsh bathroom light.

I immediately tried to cover myself but he wouldn't allow it.

Taking my hand he helped me step out, threw my towel across the edge of the tub, and pushed me down on top of it making me kneel on the floor. So now my upper body is hanging down with my breasts squashed against the side of the tub and my fat bum is pointing straight up. That also means my slit is fully exposed too.

"I suspect that my very bad girl was playing with herself in the shower and needs to be properly punished," he says, asking: "You are my naughty slut, aren't you?"

"Oh no, Sir. I'm your good girl." I gasp, already panting with excitement.

"Hmm, this rosy red backside tells a different story. It shows me that you've already had a taste of discipline recently but I think you need more – much more. What do you think, saucy brat?"

"I th-think you should give me whatever you decide I need... Sir."

He gives a satisfied rumble at both my words and the tremor in my voice.

CRACK! SMACK! His had comes down hard and my wet skin makes the sting even sharper. He continues without pause, administering a sound spanking that has me writhing with the pain and the pleasure of it. This position stretches my legs and I really feel every stroke as he pays special attention to the delicate skin where my thighs meet my bottom.

"This is what you need, isn't it?"

"Ow! Yes, yes it is."

"Maybe I should give you a few whacks with my razor strop, hmm? Do you need to have your shiny ass whipped with leather?"

My bottom is simultaneously wet yet on fire, and I'm also drowning in my own cum. Positioned over the edge of the tub means there's nothing to rub against my clit and it's aching for his touch. I feel my legs spreading of their own accord, I'm shameless and ravenous with need.

"No-no-no please don't whip me, please fuck me. Please, please, please just fuck my begging pussy. I'll be your good girl."

Derek dropped to his knees behind me and pulled off his pants. The moment his cock touched my clit I shattered into pieces. He plunged in and there we were under bright fluorescent light fucking over the edge of our bathtub.

He held onto me by my tits as he pounded hard and fast and I wiggled my hot butt for him. I actually screamed with delight when his dick hit my G-spot, up until then I wasn't even sure I had one!

He delivered a few more slaps to my stinging ass while harshly whispering in my ear:

"I'm fucking you and I'm spanking you and you're cumming because you love it, don't you? my naughty baby, my dirty little girl, my slutty wife."

"I do, Derek, I do! I love it and I love you, I love what you do to me, everything that you do to me. Promise me this forever."

He shot his hot sticky load inside me crying out: "Oh Polly, Polly, I love you so much!"

Spanking as foreplay has been a revelation to both of us.

On Monday morning Derek comes into the bathroom when he hears me turn the shower off, and he's holding a tube of numbing cream.

"Bend over the sink and I'll rub this into your skin," he says, explaining: "This will help you sit more easily at work. You don't want those co-workers of yours to see you struggling to get comfortable and start teasing you about this, right?"

"I most definitely don't!" I agree as I get into position. His touch is so gentle and the cream is soothing because my flesh is still brightly coloured. If not flaming red any more then at least a very deep, deep pink!

He doesn't say anything but from what I can see of his face in the mirror he's intently focused on his task and wearing a small smile. I realize the sight of my blushing backside gives him a great deal of satisfaction at his mastery of my body.

I almost snort out a laugh but instead tuck the thought away until I can study and reflect on it, and what meaning it might have on our future escapades, and how this idea directly impacts me.

After finishing and washing his hands Derek draws me into a soul-satisfying kiss. It's a turn-on to be naked against his fully clothed body. I had no idea I would find submission so erotic.

I always liked having plans made for me, and things thought out so I just had to follow instructions, but the feeling of being utterly helpless and at his mercy – while knowing he's going to use me to please himself – that just sends my desire skyrocketing.

No, I have no intention of sharing our weekend adventure with Cathy and Shelby. It's not that I'm ashamed well... maybe a little, because they've teased me before about Derek being older, and being put across his knee does sound kind of childish. Except there is nothing of the little girl in the way I've responded to him these past couple of days.

I never knew I had such an appetite for sex, sex, and more sex. I was practically gobbling his cock and when he pressed a finger into my anus I felt so sexy I didn't even murmur a protest. But the orgasms... shattering!

I can't believe I just kept producing more and more cum. I dripped, my clitoris was drowned, and I've been so overstimulated just crossing my legs makes me tremble. We've had more sex this weekend then we did on our honeymoon!

This foreplay spanking has certainly awakened a hunger and an itch that I never even knew existed. I don't feel browbeaten when I'm riding his cock and gasping out dirty commands like *harder, deeper, fuck me!* But I suppose what really stirs me is being dominated so decisively by Derek, my Chartered Accountant husband!

I didn't really expect any spanking play to happen during the week – although I confess I was hopeful! But when the following weekend came and went without even a suggestion of having my backside warmed I have to admit to disappointment.

A memo was sent round at work advising all unused Personal Days must be taken before month-end. That's not really giving a lot of notice, but since there are only the three of us we can work it out. Nobody wants to miss taking a day off with pay!

Only one of us can be gone per day so Cathy, since she has seniority, is taking Friday while Shelby is taking Thursday. That leaves Wednesday for me.

I was quite excited to share the news with Derek when I got home. In fact, I'm awfully tempted to ask if he might want to use this unexpected free time for some of our special play time.

"Damn, Polly. I won't be home Wednesday. I'm meeting with my boss, Andrea, to discuss my new contract."

"Oh no, can't you—"

"No way, hon. I'm hoping to negotiate a better term – in fact, I'm hoping she might offer me a partnership."

"Really? That's wonderful news, Derek."

"Awww, poor baby. I can see you're disappointed but I'll make it up to you, I promise."

"Well, I guess I can go shopping and buy myself something to cheer me up."

"Why not shop at the lingerie store and cheer both of us up?" he said with a sexy leer.

We had a normal bout of lovemaking that night and as always it was great, but I had hoped for more. I just can't bring myself to ask. I mean, we both enjoyed it so why doesn't he suggest... or better yet just grab hold of me and flip me over his knee?

He left the house for his eleven o'clock meeting this morning looking really sharp. I'm used to him being in jeans and a sweatshirt while working from home. Of course he dresses up to meet clients but most often those appointments take place when I'm at work myself. Today he's at the head office and then going on for a power lunch as he laughingly calls it.

His wears a blue shirt with a dark gray suit and his tie adds colour while matching perfectly. I can tell he's shaved with the straight razor because his skin feels extra smooth when I stroke his face while kissing him.

His shoes are polished, his slim briefcase is stylish, and he's just such a handsome man!

I dropped Derek off then came for a leisurely breakfast before getting myself ready to go shopping. I headed out to the mall that has the *Amorous Angel* lingerie shop and I'm determined to come home with something that makes me feel pretty *and* horny!

Derek's meeting with the head office executives went very well. No one has mentioned a partnership but he's feeling hopeful and fairly confident.

Right now he's waiting in the lobby for Andrea to join him. The restaurant she's chosen is only a few blocks away but she's driving them because she'll be heading out to another meeting afterwards. Since Derek and Polly only keep one car now he'll take an Uber back home.

Andrea is a good-looking woman with a no-nonsense air. She can be sharp-tongued, but also kind and considerate. Derek enjoys her company and she's always found him to be an attractive man, although too young for her. Besides, she would never get involved with an employee. A partner though... but no, he has a young wife who is chubby but very pretty.

Andrea works hard at the gym and on her treadmill at home to keep herself in trim, tip-top condition.

A valet is waiting when she exits the car and soon they're inside the bar of the posh restaurant enjoying a drink before going in to their meal. Their conversation turns back to the director's meeting and when Derek is offered the opportunity of a partnership he is deeply gratified.

"I'm glad that's out of the way so we can eat in a relaxed and friendly atmosphere," Andrea comments and Derek wholeheartedly agrees.

They talk about what Andrea's nearly grown children are doing, and that topic carries them through the forty-five minutes of lunch. Both decline coffee and after signing the bill Andrea and Derek head out. She teases him about starting a family of his own but before he can reply his phone blares with... an audio/video clip of his naked wife bent over their kitchen table while he delivers a hard hand-spanking to her rosy red bottom.

All color drains from Derek's face and with shaking hands he stabs at his phone to turn off the clip and ends up having to shut it right down. He looks into Andrea's face and sees her mouth is an O shape and her eyes are wide with shock.

He stammers out an apology and tries to explain his Smart phone is synced with his Smart TV and realizing the implications of *that* words fail him.

Andrea takes a moment to compose herself after what she's just seen and heard then placing her hand on Derek's shoulder reassures him that no harm is done, at least it didn't go off in the restaurant, and not to worry because she knows he hasn't even been married for a year yet. She smiles and surprises him with a wink before walking to her waiting car.

Derek thinks he might be sick to his stomach but decides he just needs to walk off the feeling in fresh air. Turning away from the restaurant he sets off at a brisk pace. He knows he'll come to a city park within a few blocks and can sit on a bench until he's ready to call up his ride from there.

His stride grows longer and faster as anger takes hold of his emotions and he feels it bubbling up from inside himself. He's containing his rage because he's in public but knows as soon as he gets home he will unleash it.

I'm delighted with my successful shopping trip. I finished much sooner then I thought I would, despite lingering over a coffee and pastry even though I know I don't need those calories, and soon found myself back home in the empty house.

This is unusual and feels odd because Derek is almost always at home when I am. I'm eager to know how his meeting went and hope he gets what he wants. He deserves it. I wish he'd get in touch, but I know I can't disturb him so I'll just have to be patient.

I take my purchases into the kitchen to cut the tags off and once again admire both of the sexy outfits that I bought. In fact, I think I'll put one on to surprise Derek when he gets home.

If his news is good we can celebrate and if it's bad news well, I'll do my best to make him feel better.

I pin up my hair for a tousled effect. The honey blonde is my natural color, and it's my second best feature. Stripping down I slip into my new baby-doll negligee that really enhances and shows off my best feature, or rather features. Pink is such a good color on me, it works so well with my thick, creamy skin.

The nightie comes with matching lace panties, not a thong, and I feel more comfortable wearing them. I consider putting on high heels but that might be a bit too much. Instead I put on my ballet-style slippers.

I spray on some perfume and I'm ready. Curling up on the couch with my Kindle I wait for Derek to find me here.

I finished reading my last eBook and before starting something new I turn on the TV but before I can even start flipping through the channels the screen comes alive with omigod my kitchen table spanking!

I haven't seen this video although I remember Derek taking it. Oh wow! He must have set up the screen-mirroring function so we could see it on the big TV. It's... oooh! My bottom looks so red and so sore. He's really smacking me again and again.

What a spectacle I make of myself wiggling and squirming like that. But it is pretty hot, too. I mean I'm trying to dodge his hand but at the same time I'm arching my back and my thighs keep falling open to show off my aching swollen clit.

Oh and look now Derek's in the picture too! Oh that's right, he fucked me right on the table. I just love the way he looks at me, and I love the way he's marked me with red hand-prints. I'm going to leave this on and when he comes through the door I'll hit play and he'll hear it right away. That should give him the right idea!

Hiring a ride meant Derek had to calm down for the drive home. He was so deep in his thoughts he didn't even notice when they arrived. Thanking his driver with a tip he let himself into the house and as he did so his phone buzzed with a message.

No, not a message but that video again! Stepping through his front door he heard the smack-smack sound of him spanking Polly playing on their TV. All the cooling down he'd forced on himself was gone in an instant.

Marching in to the living-room he found his bride gazing at him with a coyly demure smirk, clad in some filmy pink costume, and looking very hot and very sexy. Then his eyes were drawn to the big-screen TV and he saw himself in full color fucking her.

Anger rose up in him and he finally understood the meaning of the word rage. In those moments he saw the expression on Polly's face change from puzzlement to horror to fear.

"What's wrong, Derek? What's happened?"

She has no clue.

"That porn," he spits out, "Played over my phone when I was with my boss, you remember Andrea? Stylish, sophisticated, refined woman? Yeah, that one. That's who I was with when this started playing. Andrea saw and heard it, too.

God only knows what she thinks of me, of you, of us! She'd just offered me a partnership, too but I guess that's off the table now."

"But... but Derek how? What did I do?"

"You played this clip on the TV. It's synced to my phone and if you hadn't hit the Play button it wouldn't matter, but you did."

"But I didn't know!" she wailed.

"Yeah well... the damage is done. Fuck, fuck, fuck it's so unfair! I really worked hard for that partnership, put in the hours, brought new business to the firm, but I guess it's all for nothing now."

He clenches his fists and turns his head away from her. Deep down he understands that the video playing when he was in Andrea's company is really just a fluke, just as much his fault as hers. Polly's actions were basically an accident, and Andrea hadn't actually said she was rescinding the partnership offer...

Derek takes a couple of deep breaths to settle himself before turning back to his wife.

I've never seen Derek angry like this before. I get it, I do, I've really messed up big time. I didn't mean to but the result is still the same. And oh, what a shame! All his hard work and to think I ruined it.

He's right to be mad, he *should* be furious. He should expel his anger by disciplining me harshly.

I can feel my eyes water and my lip trembles but I bite down hard to control myself. I'm determined not to cry because this isn't about me, it's about my husband, the man I love, and all the emotions he's suffering through right now.

He's turned back towards me again and I see the hurt in his eyes. Without conscious thought I pull off my slippers and hand one to him, upside down, showing him the smooth worn leather of its sole.

Wordlessly, I undo the one ribbon holding my new baby-dolls together and toss the garment aside. His eyes automatically go to my naked breasts but I turn and kneel on the couch with my body pressed against the back.

I reach behind to pull down my panties, baring my bottom to invite his punishment, before stretching my arms to hang over the sofa back.

"I'm so, so sorry husband. I deserve whatever punishment you mete out."

"You will be sorry Pauline Jenkins! You're going to get everything you deserve and more!"

I hear a swish of air and then smack! The leather makes contact on my flesh but I can barely gasp a breath before I feel the impact of the next stroke and the next and the next. In a frenzy of spanking Derek covers every inch of my backside, each swat coming so quickly it sounds like applause.

I'd been hoping for a spanking for days but this stings so much, this is truly punishment. In no time my bum is incredibly sore and tender. I can't hold back my tears or my cries of pain. My yells of owww! and ouch! have dwindled to mewls of aiyee-ai-ai-ah! while I try to gulp in big breaths. There seems to be no time at all from one impact to the next.

This is so different from our weekend of spanking fun. This time he's really hurting me but I asked for it and I know I deserve it.

The pain is immense! Yet Derek is relentless in applying stroke after stroke, powerfully swinging his arm. I'm clutching the back of the sofa with all my strength and what a sorry sight I must be.

And then he stops. He stops but only to pull out his phone and take a couple of pictures explaining this time he's going to delete them after he's printed us each a copy - in full color and on shiny photo paper - of my blistering red bottom.

"Because in time you'll forget the pain of this spanking so the photo will serve as a reminder of your punishment at my hands... and how easily I can – and will - do it again!" he threatens.

Then he slides his hand around my pussy and slips a little in the embarrassing wetness before lifting me up on top of the couch back. I'm only balanced on my hips and start tipping over but he yanks be back in position and gripping my hair tightly holds me in place.

"School is still in session, little girl. I know you're already dripping but plan on getting even wetter because here comes your second lesson."

And, unbelievably, he starts all over again! He moves down my aching flesh to the delicate spot, my sit spot where my legs join my body, but he doesn't stop there. This pose exposes my pussy and he's making sure it gets smacked hard as well. That really hurts. After a couple of swats the slipper gets sticky so he switches to his hand.

Derek peppers me with sharp stinging smacks all over my bottom, even my inner thighs, and right down practically to my knees. All that tender skin is on fire as he spanks me thoroughly. I try to fight him but he wraps his left arm around my torso and holds me secure.

This is worse than our whole weekend's worth of foreplay spankings. He's really hurting me and he enjoys doing so, I can hear him chuckling as I yelp high-pitched screams at the pain.

"Now you're really going to get it," he says with a nasty laugh. Then he spanks just one spot, over and over again, till I'm dying from the pain before moving on to concentrate on another single spot, again repeatedly in that one spot, before moving on again. I'm shrieking with the burning agony.

This punishment is never-ending and now I'm rebelling against the unfairness of it all and say so. It's difficult to speak since I'm sobbing uncontrollably, and it's hard to be heard over the loud slapping sound of each spank.

"Derek stop! You need to stop now. This isn't fair, I didn't play that video on your phone on purpose. I didn't know that would happen, how could I? You've punished me enough."

"I'll decide when you've been punished enough, missy. As your husband, and head of this household, the amount of correction I give you is entirely my decision, not yours. This is punishment and it's supposed to hurt."

But he does stop the spanking and instead starts rubbing my exposed clit running his fingers up and down my slit, between my labia. He inserts first one then two fingers inside me while he continues the circular massaging motion with his thumb. This is his go-to move and it always works well for me. I'm shocked at the level of my arousal considering how much pain I've experienced.

"The pain enhances the pleasure, Polly. That's why you get so fucking wet when I beat your ass."

It only takes a few moments of play to bring me to the brink and then he stops. I feel movement behind me and when I turn my head I see Derek with his cock in hand – masturbating! He's left me unfinished but he jerks off on my bottom. Despite the burning of my skin I can still feel the heat of his cum. I've never felt so used! He has no consideration for me whatsoever.

"That's better," he announces in a tone I've never heard from him before. "Now I can concentrate on administering your third lesson."

He slaps his hand down and smears his ejaculate all over my ass, I feel it sticky and warm as it drips down. This degradation brings fresh tears to my eyes. Then pulling me down on the seat of the couch he tells me to get my butt upstairs and lie face down on our bed.

"And *RUN!*" he shouts.

I try, but I'm stiff from being bent over so awkwardly, sore with an extremely painful bottom, and my panties are still around my knees. I manage to climb about six stairs before he's on me, pressing me down and roughly groping me all over in a grabby way that feels nasty even though I'm so turned on.

My body is aroused but my mind has hated every minute of this and I'm wailing in protest. When he delivers several more stinging blows and orders me to hurry up I struggle to comply.

Derek climbs the stairs slowly. All those blog posts he read from people, supposedly women, with usernames like *Happily Spanked Wife* or *Proudly Paddled* talk about how emotionally comforting the Domestic Discipline lifestyle is. They claim the structure of being properly and painfully punished when they transgress makes them feel loved, safe, and secure.

He doubts if Polly is feeling that way right now. He knows he's gone overboard, in fact he's gone way, way too far. He never meant to ever spank her as punishment, it's just that she invited him so temptingly to slipper her luscious naked bottom when he was already very, very angry with her.

Daylight shining down on the stairs from the window on the landing shows how painfully red he's beaten Polly's behind and it's unnerved him. The realization of how much she must hurt, both physically and emotionally, fills him with a deep shame that he could treat his wife this way.

Reading about spanking had led him to BDSM sites where he learned new things - some frightening but some intriguing - and he had planned on tormenting her further but now he's shocked himself out of that black place his mind had descended into.

Even before he gets to the bedroom he can hear the heart-wrenching sound of Polly's deep sobs. He finds her lying on the bed, as he ordered, face down and naked. The sight of her body stirs him, but the mournful sounds from her repress any budding urge, and he abandons his idea to tie her spreadeagled to the bedposts before attacking her bottom again. She's crying so pitifully. His poor young wife.

He goes into the *en suite* to get the *aloe vera* lotion and returns to smooth it on her sore flesh. She flinches when she feels him sit beside her and that fearful reaction stabs right through his heart. He makes shushing sounds as he pours the cool lotion on her burning skin. With the lightest of touches covers every inch that flames red, from her waist to her knees.

Derek is utterly filled with a remorse that he can't verbalize. Probably just as well since there are no words to explain or justify or excuse. So he uses the salve to ease her physical pain then he rubs her back and shoulders, nuzzles her neck, and angles her tear-stained face so he can kiss her lips.

She whispers *I'm sorry, Derek* and he feels like a monster.

Lying down on his back he pulls Polly on top and wraps his arms around her, holding her close. Polly lays her head on his chest, listening to his quick heartbeat, while Derek strokes her hair. They lie quietly like that until Polly falls into an exhausted sleep.

Derek is wondering if Polly does feel *loved and cared for*, or if she's just thankful he's stopped hurting her? She might not realize he stopped because he was sickened by his own behavior. She might think this is part of the whole punishment discipline, the aftercare.

Derek's demon is firmly pushed back deep down in his psyche. He acknowledges to himself that he has violent primal urges, and that reading and looking at pictures about this sort of thing on the Internet

probably stimulated them, made them seem acceptable – even normal
– but he doesn't care. That's not the person he wants to be, not the
husband his wife should have.

He never meant for this to happen, and doesn't think they'll ever talk
about it.

I wakened at dusk, and could tell by Derek's breathing that he was
asleep but he woke as soon as I moved. Lifting up on my arms I was able
to look at his face and he met my gaze without any expression. I have
no idea what he's thinking but it doesn't look like he's mad any more.

Then he gives me a small smile and I kiss him. He slides me off his body
and onto the bed, still on my stomach. He sits up and pushes my legs
forward so I'm on my knees with my hips raised just enough for his
hand to slip into my slit and start stroking.

I no longer feel the least bit horny but he caresses my clit, kisses my
thighs, and blows on my bottom until it goosebumps so it doesn't take
long to get me wet again. Soon I'm moving to the rhythm of his fingers
inside me and his thumb massaging me and I cry out with pleasure. This
is the husband I know, my Derek.

I slump back down but now he's pulling me higher on my knees so he
can slip down beneath me to lick my sensitive clit. His tongue swirls me
like I'm delicious and his murmurs of appreciation and approval have
me gyrating back and forth. It's like my clit is fucking his tongue.

The most marvellous sensations flutter up and down my body from my
sensitive nub to my nipples and back again. Rippling waves of pleasure
at my husband's loving skill.

I've lifted up on my hands as well and he reaches up to fondle my breasts and rub my hard nipples with his fingertips. Thrills runs through me as Derek finds joy in my body, and emotionally I'm so happy that we're in sync again.

This time the orgasm fills me with a cold sensation that burns as it draws out a long, deep groan from me. He scoots up along my body until I can feel his cock pushing its way inside. I spread wide to welcome him and, careful not to touch any of my sore spots, he holds me steady while his hips buck and he drives in deeply.

Soon I'm riding him with enthusiasm and though I feel pain each time my inner thighs land back down on his groin the pleasure is worth it. I bring him to climax first, feeling great satisfaction when he calls out my name in a ragged voice, and then I join him in ecstasy. I spasm again, so many orgasms!

Exhausted and satisfied we collapse in a sweaty embrace. My limbs feel full of water instead of bones. I'm weak and drained from the exquisite pleasure of repeated shattering delight.

After a few moments Derek rubs my back and asks how I feel.

I reply, with complete honesty: "Hungry."

He chuckles and tells me to just relax, to nap some more if I like, and he'll bring up a supper of scrambled eggs and toast.

"Perfect," I answer sleepily.

I have to go to work the next day. It's office policy that if we cancel either the day before or after our Personal Day we won't get paid for it.

So, once again Derek helps coat my bottom with numbing cream and suggests I wear at least two pairs of underwear for extra padding and comfort.

"What about those red velvet panties you have?" he asks.

I have to think for a minute before I realize he means the velour ensemble I bought for Christmas. Yes, they'd work but Christmas was months ago and I've put on a few more pounds since then. Honestly, I'm so lucky Derek's in love with my big boobs that he forgives the matching belly and butt! I do manage with the extra undies, despite feeling a bit like a diapered baby. It certainly does make sitting down more comfortable, and my wide long skirt hides everything.

We haven't spoken about the spanking he gave me yesterday. It was so much more than just a spanking, it was a brutal punishment. It was like Derek unleashed something dark and cruel inside himself.

I suspect my submissive invitation was partly to blame. The way I so subserviently offered up my naked backside to him must have encouraged an urge to dominate me. At first I thought he was going to do even more. He seemed oblivious to the pain I was suffering, as if it was only incidental to the lust of rage or whatever it was he experienced, but luckily he didn't go any further.

I also think he might have given himself a bit of a fright too, because he's been so solicitous and tender towards me. I got through my two weekdays at work and then had a restful weekend.

Andrea phoned to confirm his partnership offer and work out details of the proposal. Derek's relief was immense and on Saturday night he took me out to dinner at a swanky restaurant to celebrate. I got dressed up in something tastefully low-cut, and styled my hair in a sexy updo that had him staring and complimenting me all night.

Now we're back home and it seems like a good opportunity to talk. We're both happily full from dinner, and made mellow by the wine, so I brew a pot of coffee. We held hands the whole way home in the Uber – Derek believes in the zero tolerance alcohol and driving policy – and we will make love tonight but first I want us to clear the air.

Derek has always taken charge of our lives and I've been happy to go along with that, but we need to have this talk. I really, really feel it's important to us, and our future together, to express all the embarrassing and shaming emotions and thoughts. Get them out in the open and take away their harmful power. I need to be strong enough to push for answers if necessary. Because it matters.

I load up our coffee and fixings on a tray and carry it into the living-room. I've added some cookies, too, because something sweet to nibble on makes the coffee taste better. No doubt it's this kind of thinking that explains why I'm fifteen *or more* pounds overweight. Derek loves my home-baking but he has an enviable metabolism.

"I'd like to talk about what happened between us on Wednesday, Derek." I see him frown and hasten to add: "Not to complain, but to understand. However, first I want to know what my third lesson was supposed to be?"

"What do you mean?" he questions back, and from the way he fails to meet my gaze I know he's deliberately being evasive.

"When you finished with me here, on this couch, you ordered me upstairs to get *my third lesson* – that's what you said – and please don't pretend you've forgotten, hon. I think it's important that we're completely honest with each other. So, tell me what else did you have in mind for me?"

Derek actually blushes! I didn't know he could.

"Polly, I am so sorry about how far things went, no, how far *I* took them. I'm 100% responsible for what happened. I need you to forgive me, and for both of us to forget what happened and move on."

He's so earnest but I'm not letting him off the hook, this is too important to me and to our marriage.

"Of course I forgive you, Derek, just as you forgave me, but I'm definitely not ready to forget without at least understanding exactly what happened and why. So, what was your plan for *lesson number three?*"

He looks down at his coffee and quietly answers: "Bondage."

"Bondage? Okay... but I need details of what exactly that would have entailed."

He looks at me now with a scowl that's supposed to intimidate but I'm adamant in finding out exactly how far he wanted to go.

I guess he sees the determination in my face because he sighs gustily and explains: "I was going to take four of your long scarves, long so that you'd have a bit of room to move to, to let me see you squirm, when I tied you spreadeagled, face down, to the bedposts. I was going to slide all the pillows under your hips so you'd be lifted up and open for me. Like, helpless.

I wasn't going to spank you any more, or at least that wasn't my plan, but I did want to admire what I'd already done. I wanted to stroke your red, swollen skin and feel the heat while you cried to be soothed.

My plan was to use that vibrator your friend Cathy from work gave you as a Secret Santa gift? I was going to torment you with orgasm after orgasm. I wanted to watch you convulse in your restraints... and

I wanted to hear you cry for me to fuck you, beg and plead to feel my cock inside you."

"Oh. That doesn't sound like a bad lesson, actually," I say with a smile.

"Except I was going to fuck your ass and that would have been anal rape because I don't think that's something you want to do—"

I gasp and he reaches for my hands and holds them tightly, saying: "Oh Polly! I'm so sorry. I can't believe I had these thoughts. You're right, the bondage and vibrator duo could be fun foreplay, pleasurable for both of us, but I wanted to keep going until I'd made it something nasty and dark."

"Because your beast was let out and I'm partly to blame for that—"

"No, you had no idea that video was synced to the TV and my phone. You're truly not to blame."

"No, I didn't mean that. Although thank you for acknowledging... anyhow, I meant maybe my very submissive behaviour enticed your beast to come out and play. His version of play, that is."

"But that's exactly what *shouldn't* have happened! When you're weak and vulnerable it makes me feel big and strong and I *do* want to protect and nurture you and care for you but... I never knew I had a beast inside – that's a good description, by the way – until he came roaring out to dominate, crush, and harm. Until that happened I never even knew he was there."

"So I think it's good we learned about this aspect of you, right? and we can set limits in case he's triggered again."

"I did read about using a safe word, and it's usually a color. Like red means *stop immediately*, and green means it's still okay, *keep going*.

That's for people who are deliberately testing their limits of pain and delivering pain. But I don't want that for us."

"No, I don't either but... Derek, are you saying that you want to have anal sex but have been suppressing that desire?"

"Well... men talk, you know. They talk about how after she's had a couple of kids their wife's vagina gets stretched out a bit, but it's their kids, and it's them that caused the problem, so they can't complain but they talk about how their wife's ass is so much tighter.

So, sure it sounds interesting. Although I have nothing to complain about with you Polly you're well... as tight as a man could ever want."

Saying *gee, thanks* doesn't seem appropriate but his roundabout conversation does need a response: "But you'd like to experiment?"

He runs his hands through his thick hair, pushing it up off his face and looking ten years younger, my handsome husband can always raise my heart-rate. I don't often see Derek struggling with words and looking so vulnerable.

"In my mind, my fantasies, I guess, it's always forced because I never thought we'd ever be talking about this. Maybe even considering this... because it's always been a dark desire I've pushed it down."

I capture his hand again and looking him straight in the eye I let him know that I'm perfectly willing to try anal sex so long as he goes slow and promises to penetrate me as gently as he can.

"For sure, hon. I'll use lots of lube, and if it hurts you too much I'll stop right away."

"And will you still enjoy it if it isn't a rough, raping act?"

"God yes. I'm sure if we can both orgasm with me teasing your clit while my dick's deep in your ass I'll never need to have those brutal thoughts again."

"It's a date," I say with a nervous laugh. Okay, I'm really apprehensive about this but women talk too and I just might be one of those lucky enough to enjoy it. My bum does seem to be one of my more powerful erogenous zones!

"Going back to our original conversation Derek, now it's my turn to be completely honest with you."

I force myself to look into his eyes but I know that now I'm the one who is blushing up a storm. I can feel the burn come right up from my chest.

"Derek, making myself vulnerable and exposed to your anger was such an incredible turn-on. I knew you were going to spank me hard and it was going to sting like hell but I wanted to feel that. Not the actual pain but the fact that it was being inflicted on me by you. That I provoked and angered you, my husband, to that point of total domination.

I started to feel like I deserved everything I was getting and... this is awkward, but well... it was feeling *right*. Something inside me must crave punishment because it was being satisfied.

The feeling of me being utterly subservient, slavish, to you. That got me so hot. In fact, just talking about it now is making me wet.

But the reality did go too far because it hurt too much and I no longer felt I was safe in the hands of my husband. Up until that point I wanted you to use me however you pleased but then I got scared.

So, I guess I'm the submissive type in my head: the words, the ideas, the thoughts turn me on, but in practical terms not so much."

"And I'm getting turned on just thinking about pounding into you and having you accept it all – the slaps, the love-bites, grabbing handfuls of flesh and squeezing, talking dirty – and forcing you to tell me that I'm your one and only. I really love to hear you say that I'm the best you ever had, that I own you and you love it."

"Cookies!" I cry out.

Derek is confused, his mind still locked into his fantasy scenario. "What?"

"Let's do some role-playing and we'll make our safe word cookies. Because we might use the words *red* and *stop* in our sex-play without really meaning it. But I don't imagine we'll ever accidentally scream out *cookies.*"

"Well, sure if that's what you want to use—"

"Derek, I never want to be in another Wednesday situation, but I do want us to explore your desires. Especially since they fit so nicely with mine. I mean, you want to dominate and I want to be submissive, but you need to control your inner beast."

"Oh Polly, that sounds... that sounds wonderful, truly. Because I'd love to tie you up—"

"I would love it too!" I interrupt happily.

"Oh wow. So maybe it's okay to have a beast that can be tamed. Now I'm wondering about the kind of man Robert Louis Stevenson was..."

"Who's that?"

"The man who wrote Dr. Jekyll and Mr. Hyde."

"Oh, was that a book? I've heard those names but I thought they were real people."

Suddenly he laughs and pulls me across the couch into his arms in a cuddly embrace saying:

"Oh my sweet, young bride!"

We haven't experimented yet. Derek has been very busy with lots of trips to head office getting his partnership sorted. He's so excited about it and I'm proud of him and happy for him.

After that video clip she saw I bet skinny Andrea's given him one or two speculative looks – I know a cougar when I see one! – but he's never said anything. For such a handsome man my husband is quite oblivious.

We share Derek's big desktop computer but still, I waited until I was alone at home before logging on and checking his browser history. I wanted to know what he saw and read in those BDSM sites. He told me himself that he visited these places so it's not like I'm spying on him, but I want to be on my own when I look at them.

I'm so glad I was by myself. Following his trail I went to sites about *Domestic Discipline* which led to other similar sites and blogs. I ended up spending over an hour reading posts, guest posts, and readers' questions. It sounded pretty awful to me, some of the stories even involved the shaming and exposure of wives in public. But then I realized a lot was probably just bragging and fantasizing.

I have to admit I did get turned on by the pictures. Some were drawings but most were photos showing women's bare bottoms in various shades of pink and red, and usually including a man's hand holding a spanking instrument.

I'd always thought of spanking as an over-the-knee paddling by hand, but much of what I was looking at were beatings for punishment, not sexual spankings, or at least not to my mind. I prefer my definition of the act.

I also followed his browsing path to sites on bondage and vibrators and some unusual tools-of-the-trade. It was truly an education. A few things turned my stomach but overall I was in awe at just how popular kink must be to have such a wide market. It's not dark and nasty – or not necessarily, I guess for some the dirtier the better! but it's part of the human psyche and it can't be easily dismissed.

When I told Derek that I got awfully aroused by my pleasure spanking he eagerly agreed that he'd enjoyed the whole experience that weekend. We're both turned on by our Dominant vs Submissive fantasies which are so darn vanilla *I'm learning the terminology!* compared to real D/s stuff and that suits us.

Threats spoken – whispered - by my husband like: *you're gonna get it now naughty girl,* and *my hand is just itching to spank your bare bottom rosy red,* stimulate a strong response making me hot and horny. Those couple of days of pleasure spanking were a revelation. So much pleasure from me acting saucy and sassy until Derek forced me to feel the palm of his hand on my behind, both of us enjoying my *correction.*

Going forward our fun playtime will include spanking, blowjobs, bondage, a vibrator, and lots of orgasms for both of us!

Eventually we might investigate a few of those BDSM websites together, but for now I'm sure our fantasy role-playing, mixed with our regular gentle lovemaking, will keep us both well-satisfied.

Also, I told Derek that if he ever gets really angry with me again he should get it out of his system by taking me to bed and fucking me senseless. Punishing my helpless cunt with his angry cock. He loves it when I talk that way - so long as we're alone in our own home, that is! No more real punishment spankings, only the erotic kinds with lots of trash talk for our mutual pleasure.

We're scheduling our fantasy play-dates - my husband is an accountant, after all - for every other Friday, payday! and this gives us both something to look forward to with anticipation and trepidation. Just talking about it with him gets me horny but he insists that waiting will make us both appreciate our playtime even more.

First though, on the weeknights leading up we'll tell each other stories. These scenarios will give the background to the punishment, and the motivation of the participants. The actual role-playing will be pretty one-dimensional because we'll both be excited for the action to begin and won't want to waste time explaining ourselves!

We plan to act out some strong-male-and-helpless-female roles like:

Male Cop and Female Driver,

Male Security Guard and Female Shoplifter,

BMOC and the Co-Ed,

and more.

Derek says: "I've worked out *a cop and speeding motorist* story for our first scenario. So when you get home from work on Friday I'll ask you for *your licence and registration* and you'll know you're on a lonely stretch of highway and I'm the cop who has caught you speeding, and you're the driver willing to do *anything* to avoid getting a ticket."

"Oooh, I like it. Tell me the story now so I'll know what to do."

Cop Stops Speeder Who Will Lose Her Licence With One More Ticket

Sitting in his vehicle Highway Patrolman Dennis "Denny" Callaghan, who has excellent eyesight, spots the female driver of the car he's just pulled over undo the top button of her shirt... and then two more.

He smiles to himself and hopes she's young and pretty.

Trying to control his swagger he approaches the car, a sporty little Miata convertible, and discovers she is neither of those things. She's a drop-dead gorgeous woman in her late thirties. Ten years older than him, and in her sexual prime.

The cleavage she's displaying is certainly worth looking at. Her breasts are full and round with the nipples clearly showing hard through the gauzy fabric of her blouse.

"Officer! How fast was I going? It couldn't have been too fast, could it?" She's all wide blinking eyes and a sexy pout, playing him - *or trying to!*

Officer Denny Callaghan replies with the standard: "Licence and registration, Ma'am," holding out his hand.

She inhales a deep breath, well aware of the wonderful things that does to her chest but she can't see his eyes behind those mirrored sunglasses and his face isn't giving anything away.

As she reaches across to open her glove-box he admires the suppleness of her body, and the gentle curve of her spine. He'd like to see the rest of the package. She turns back to hand him the documents and runs the tip of her tongue across her top lip.

"You were doing 75 in a 55 zone. That's twenty over the limit, Mrs..." he glances down at her licence, "Mrs. Wilson."

"Oh it's Miss, I'm not married, Officer."

"Please step out of the vehicle, Miss."

She obviously sees this command as an opportunity to employ her charms against him because she hooks a finger to lift the hem of her skirt and when she swings open the door he gets a good look at long, tanned legs and a lot of naked thigh. To be sure he's watching closely she gasps *Oh!* and makes an obvious point of covering up as she stands up.

Officer Denny Callaghan is definitely not disappointed once he gets the full view of Miss Wilson.

"Have you been drinking today, Miss?"

"Oh no, Officer. Well, just an Orange Blossom at brunch. You know, champagne and orange juice? I just had one well.. maybe two? But they're mostly orange juice so..."

"I need you to assume the position."

Miss Wilson looks totally perplexed.

"Put your hands on the hood of the car and spread your legs. I need to pat you down for weapons or contraband."

"I don't have any—"

"I don't like repeating myself, Miss." growls Officer Denny Callaghan.

Miss Wilson feels a tingle run right through her erogenous zones at his steely tone. His face looks so stern, too. But despite his expression she can see that he's a handsome young man with a buff body.

She turns awkwardly in her strappy high heels since the side of this lonely stretch of highway is made up of fine gravel, not pavement. Miss Wilson has to bend right over to place her hands flat on her low-slung two-seater.

She senses the cop right behind her and then feels his large hands give her a firm frisking from her throat, all around both breasts including her hard nipples, her belly, bottom, thighs, and then slowly stroking down each bare leg and up again, up under her skirt, cupping the roundest part of her ass, then moving between her legs. His hands linger awhile and she's sure she must be wet and he can feel it.

"Officer... Sir," Miss Wilson says in a breathy voice, "Please don't write me up. I'll do anything... anything at all, whatever you want. I really, really can't get another speeding ticket."

She turns to face him but stumbles and he has to pull her tight against his body to keep her upright. He looks down at this sexy prize, locked within his arms, and sees she's trembling. She nibbles at her lower lip, beseeching him with big eyes before slowly sliding down to kneel before him.

She finishes unbuttoning her blouse to show off her lovely tits in a low-cut bra. She opens it from a front clasp and her breasts spring free, big dark nipples proudly hard. She presses them against the zipper of his fly, fondling herself and his erection at the same time.

He quickly frees his cock and she buries it between her full, round boobs then, still holding him in place within her soft mounds, she licks his tip and then takes him in her mouth. Reaching around she grabs hold of his ass and pulls him tight against her while she expertly sucks his dick.

She flicks along his length with her tongue, sucking in her cheeks so his entire cock: head and the whole shaft, is caressed by her warm, wet mouth. Miss Wilson knows exactly what she's doing and how to do it best. Her head bobs up and down and his hips soon pick up the same rhythm, thrusting deeper into her throat.

Sensing he's near climax she pulls free and demands: "No speeding ticket, right?"

"Right!" groans Officer Denny Callaghan then pushes himself back in her mouth and she quickly brings him to completion, swallowing down the cum that pulsates out of him. When he's finished she leans back and looks up at him with a self-satisfied smirk. She's really good at giving head and she knows it.

He takes her hands and lifts her up, turning her around so she's leaning back against his chest while his hands roam all over her bare breasts, tweaking her still hard nipples.

"We have another issue to address, Miss." He rumbles in her ear as one hand slips down inside her panties and his fingers play in her wet folds of her slit. Her breathing quickens as she says:

"What issue is that, Officer?"

"That would be the crime of bribery, Miss."

She squeaks out a *Wh-what?* just as he pulls her hands behind her back and snaps his handcuffs around her wrists.

"Bribing a police officer is a very serious offence that requires a severe punishment."

"Oh please no! I'll lose my licence if I get another ticket! Please, please what can I do?" cries Miss Wilson.

Officer Denny Callaghan loves to hear this proud woman, so confident and assured, begging him for mercy. She figured that blow job got her off the hook but he has no intention of letting her off so lightly. Not after that stunt she pulled just when he was ready to explode in her mouth.

Grabbing her arms he pushes her towards the patrol car saying: "This offence calls for corporal punishment, and by time I'm done administering it you'll be wishing you could have had a ticket instead!"

He just loves the sight of her heavy naked tits swinging as she staggers on her high-heels. He almost wishes a car would drive by slowing down to could get a good look at his trophy and wishing they were him! but no, he doesn't want to share.

He opens the back door of the car to slide in then pulls her across his lap. She attempts to protest but she's half-naked with her hands cuffed behind her back so there's nothing she can actually do to stop him. This time *he's* the one with the upper hand and he's going to use it – hard and firm! She's at his mercy and they both know it.

"The back-seats in these cruisers are nice and roomy so I can get comfortably settled in for a lengthy session. Mmm-mmm, I'm looking forward to this! When is the last time you had your ass tanned, Miss Wilson?"

"Oh please don't do this Officer, please, please don't spank me!"

Officer Denny Callaghan rubs his hand over her backside, massaging and pinching as though searching for the best spot to begin.

"You're definitely going to be spanked, Miss Wilson, but if you co-operate and answer my questions – in fact, do everything I tell you to do – then I *might* go easier on you. Now, when is the last time you were spanked?"

"I, I don't know... um, when I was a kid."

Now he pushes her skirt up well past her waist and enjoys seeing her goosebumped flesh peeking out from the edge of her panties.

"Who spanked you? Parents? Brother? Teacher?"

"My babysitter."

"Ahhh, male or female?"

"Female."

He rubs her panty-clad bottom, savoring the look and feel of it. Now he's slipped his fingers into the elastic waistband of her expensive panties and is slowly tugging the silky fabric down over her plump derriere, asking:

"Did she spank you on your bare bottom?"

Miss Wilson gives a high-pitched, breathy scream: "Oh please don't pull down my panties!"

Officer Denny Callaghan just chuckles, he wants her to fully experience the humiliation of her vulnerable position, and continues to slowly torment her until her bottom is fully bared to his gaze and, as she will soon find out, to his heavy hand. Her smooth round globes are tantalizing. He can't wait to see them wobble under his masterly strokes.

"Answer me!"

She can feel his hand hovering over her naked flesh and is quivering in anticipation but he decides to draw out her torment for a few moments more.

"No, it was over my pyjamas!"

"Well a proper spanking should always be applied to bare skin so after all these years you're finally going to get the paddling you deserve."

Officer Denny Callaghan begins the spanking with steady firm strokes smacking every inch of Miss Wilson's squirming bottom with rhythmic strokes. She tries to keep herself under control, not wanting to add to her shame, but can't help wriggling her ass because his punishing hand really hurts.

"Do you deserve this?"

She twists and turns and squeals.

"Do you?" he asks again, hitting her harder.

"Yes! Yes, Officer, I deserve it."

"Have you learned your lesson?"

"Oh, absolutely. Yes, you can stop now, I'll be good."

"No, I'm not convinced. Your ass is rosy but I'm sure I can get it a much deeper shade of red."

She kicks her legs but he just chuckles at her antics. He is a very strong young man and she is no match for him. He has the stamina to do a thorough job, and he's enjoying himself immensely. He's happy to devote as much time and effort as needed to ensure Miss Wilson's spanking is a memorable one – for both of them!

The occasional car drives by but seeing the police cruiser already in attendance no one stops. A child looking out the back window comments to his parent – who suddenly slowed right down below the speed limit – that the policeman was giving the lady a spanking but he was told not to make up stories.

"I had a babysitter who used to spank me," Officer Denny Callaghan muses, "and I vowed to myself I'd get back at her someday. That never happened, I never got her across my knee, so I guess you – or rather your poor sore bum – Miss Wilson, will have to bear the brunt of my revenge. By proxy, so to speak."

He increases the speed and intensity of his swats and the pain is agonizing. Since every inch of bouncing bottom is already a fiery red each new stroke is landing on a tender spot.

"Oh! Ow, ow! Officer please! No more. Oooh! Ow-ow-ow!"

As Officer Denny Callaghan's hand keep beating a tattoo on her rapidly darkening flesh Miss Wilson is shimmying her hips and her delicious behind dances for his entertainment. The sight just spurs him on to increase the tempo.

In addition to the pleasure of hearing her gasp, moan, and beg, all of her writhing against his groin has aroused the young man. He slips a finger into her slit and immediately his excited dick demands to be sheathed in that hot wet pussy. Reluctantly, because he has reveled in the sight, sound and feel of spanking Miss Wilson, he has to stop the punishment to lift her up and onto his hard cock.

He's delighted to feel the heat of her well-spanked bottom on his bare thighs and he is soon grabbing hold of handfuls of tender hot flesh. With her arms cuffed behind her back her breasts are thrust forward and bouncing freely, they're so big that's got to be painful too. He frees one of his hands to massage her swollen breasts while pumping her up and down along his shaft.

She's sobbing from the pain but delirious from the pleasure. Miss Wilson has never been spanked by a boyfriend and never knew what a turn-on it is. The pain was dreadful but the heat it generated has left her dripping with hungry lust.

First, well-spanked and now well-fucked. He adds to her humiliation by wiping away a tear drop saying:

"I've made you leak from your eyes and your cunt, naughty Miss Wilson! The only thing left now is for you to thank me for giving you this discipline you've sorely needed," he laughs at his joke: "and sorely got!"

She gasps and as her orgasm takes her in flight screams out:

"Thank you! Thank you! Thank you!"

After joining her in their mutual ecstasy Officer Denny Callaghan cuddles his prisoner till their breathing returns to normal then he releases her and helps her to exit the police car.

She should be a sorry sight with her eye makeup smeared, lipstick chewed off, and hair mussed but her beautiful face is still stunning. Despite looking so dishevelled, with her bra and blouse pulled down her arms to her handcuffed wrists, her bare breasts look magnificent. With her skirt pulled up around her waist he has an exciting view of her gently curving belly, smooth rounded thighs, a naked mound with soaked clit and cum-filled pussy, and long shapely legs.

He turns her around to unlock the handcuffs but pauses for a moment to admire his handiwork. Her bottom looks as luscious and red as a polished apple. When he touches her she flinches but soon wiggles back into his cupped hands. They stand there like that for a few moments, him enjoying the heat and her enjoying the caress, before she turns and kisses his cheek.

"You're welcome," he says in reply.

He frees her, helps her pull her clothes back into place, and escorts her back to her car. Once he sees her safely buckled in with the engine purring he steps back but not before adding:

"Today's Tuesday which means you'll still be sore tomorrow and probably the next day too, but I'm sure you'll be ready for another hard spanking and fucking by Friday so I'll be here waiting."

Her eyes widen and her mouth shapes itself into an O of surprise. She says nothing but driving away he sees her eyes staring at him speculatively in her rear-view mirror as she shifts in her seat, trying to get comfortable. Officer Denny Callaghan feels confident he'll see her again.

Meanwhile, he has to find the panties he ripped from her and tossed somewhere in the backseat of the cruiser. A pleasantly musky-scented souvenir.

"Oh hon, I'm looking forward to doing that! A blow job, a spanking, and hot sex!"

"Don't forget about the handcuffs."

"Omigod no, can't forget those!"

"And the very high-heels that make you wobble."

"Wobble right into your strong manly embrace."

"You mean like this?" and then Derek cuddles and kisses me and we head upstairs for an early night.

After a lot of sexy fun on our Special Friday – both of us really getting into our roles and hamming it up - we've settled back to our regular routine. Now it's my turn to come up with our next story.

Guilty Nurse Lies to Doctor About Quitting Smoking

Talk about good news/bad news! thinks Nurse Ivy as handsome Doctor Shane stands so close to her that she can feel his warm breath as he sniffs her hair.

Nurse Ivy is working the night shift at the Clinic which is an easy, but boring, job. Her patients are all topped up with their medication and tucked up in their beds. Other then walking the rounds every few hours she's got plenty of time to update her charts and complete her reports. All the boring paperwork.

That's why it's so delightful to see Doctor Shane come through the door just after midnight. Of course it's great to see him at any time with his thick blond hair, bright blue eyes, and killer smile. But for the them to be here together, to spend time alone, well... bonus! She's always had a thing for him and the two of them have begun that age-old dance of flirtation.

The bad news is that he's close enough to smell the tobacco of a sneaked ciggie and is about to reprimand her for smoking since she promised she would quit and now she's going to have to lie about it.

"Nurse Ivy, do I smell cigarette smoke on you?" says Doctor Shane is an uninflected tone of voice that carries a hint of threat.

"You might, Doctor Shane, because I did wheel old Mr Jenkins outside for his allotted bedtime cigarette, and maybe some of the smoke got caught in my hair," replies Nurse Ivy, lying smoothly.

Doctor Shane studies her face for a moment but she looks back at him innocently with guileless eyes. He isn't fooled, though. He roughly pulls her face close and bruises her lips with an open-mouthed kiss. His tongue swirls around and then he pushes her away with narrowed eyes.

"And did you lick the ashtray too, Nurse Ivy? Because that's what your mouth tastes like."

"Oh, Doctor Shane I—"

"Don't lie again, Nurse Ivy. You promised me you would quit smoking and when I asked about it you swore you had. You lied then and you're lying now."

Damn! he's really angry with me, she thinks. Reaching out to touch his arm Nurse Ivy turns on the charm. She thrusts her chest forward, nibbles on her bottom lip, and lets her eyes fill with tears as she murmurs,

"Please Doctor Shane, can't you forgive me this one time?"

"A woman with a cigarette in her mouth looks like a cheap slut, Nurse Ivy. If that's how you want me to see you then that's how I'll treat you. I'm going to do my rounds now and when I return I want you changed out of your uniform and into a one of the old Candy Striper uniforms. I know there are some still hanging in the cloakroom. You put on one of those and nothing else and be waiting for me in the Doctor's Lounge."

"But Doctor, those were made for girls to wear, I won't fit into one of them."

"Then you really will look slutty, won't you? Don't worry, I'll give you something to put in your mouth to suck on and that will complete the tarty look!"

Nurse Ivy's generous breasts don't fit in the faded old dress so she has to leave half the buttons undone. It's so short it doesn't fully cover her rear and it's too tight to pull down any further. She's naked underneath and suspects it won't be long until all the buttons pop loose and expose her all the way down.

She knows what Doctor Shane wants so she tries to alleviate his anger by being ready for him. She kneels down and places her palms on her thighs like a good obedient girl. This position forces the hem of the dress to push up baring more than half her behind.

It's uncomfortable waiting like this but she figures if she does a good job sucking his dick that he'll forgive her for lying to him. She truly does want to quit smoking, but some days it's really hard and she gives in to the temptation to have a few puffs.

Hearing his footsteps echoing down the hall she straightens up and licks her lips in anticipation. When he opens the door his eyes widen and the hint of a smile touches the curve of his lips. He slowly walks all around her, getting an eyeful, before saying:

"Suddenly pretending to be a good girl, hmm Nurse Ivy? I appreciate the attempt but we both know you're just a dirty slut who should have her mouth washed out with soap but instead will get it fucked by her angry doctor with a cock that needs satisfying."

He unzips his pants and frees his thick penis. It's already tumescent and he strokes it till the end glistens with precum. Then he holds the back of Nurse Ivy's head and thrusts himself into her open mouth.

She immediately starts working her lips and tongue while he pushes in deeper and deeper until he's reached all the way to the back of her throat. She starts to gag but gets herself under control when he glares down.

Now he's gripping her chin with his other hand to hold her firmly in place while thrusting in and out. He instructs her to fondle his nut sack. Nurse Ivy complies and the feel of her cool hands tickling and caressing shoots his semen out across her tongue and down her throat.

She's gulping air and hot cum and swallowing everything.

"Does that wipe the taste of tobacco from your mouth, Nurse Ivy?" he asks.

"Yes, Doctor Shane, it does," she says nodding eagerly.

"Well next time you want to smoke think about blowing me instead. I'm sure we'll almost always be able to manage a quick trip to the linen closet or sneak out to my car. Substitution is an excellent way to wean off your bad habit. Got it?"

"Oh yes, Doctor Shane. Thank you for caring."

He studies her a moment suspiciously but decides she's being sincere.

"Now unfortunately that's insufficient compensation for your lying to me - twice. For that, you need a severe punishment."

Nurse Ivy's eyes are huge and her mouth forms an O as she quavers:

"Wh-what do you mean, Doctor Shane?"

Stepping back he tucks himself back into his pants and reaches out a hand to pull her to her feet. He gets a full view of her luscious body trapped in the tight fabric of the Candy Striper's uniform.

Leading her to a couch he sits down and pulls her across his lap. He chuckles at the sight of her mostly bared bottom before pushing her dress right up over her round behind. Now she's completely naked from the waist down, and he's heard the material stretch and tear as the buttons pop off meaning her breasts have pushed free.

He grabs at her ass and her tits while telling her she's a dirty little girl who's going to be thoroughly punished for her naughtiness.

"A good old-fashioned bare-bottom spanking will teach you not to lie to me."

"Oh Doctor Shane I'm so sorry, please don't do—"

But Nurse Ivy doesn't even get to finish the sentence before a firm hand smacks down on her bare flesh... and strikes again and again and again.

"Just lovely, Nurse Ivy. A lovely derriere that's becoming a pretty shade of pink. But I'm not a *rosé* man so let's see about doing a proper job and turning this ass bright red."

He's relentless in administering a hard, harsh spanking on her helpless, half-naked body, making sure to fully cover both cheeks with punishing strokes. He applies a dozen or so haphazardly and then another dozen alternating from one cheek to the next. The roundest, extremely sensitive part of her bottom gets the most attention.

Nurse Ivy wriggles and kicks but she can't avoid the stinging swats that repeatedly follow one after the other. She's embarrassed to be yelping with the pain but her bottom is really burning. She hasn't been spanked since childhood, and even if she had ever imagined being put across handsome Doctor Shane's knee it would be for a sexy fun spanking, not this scorcher.

Because he's a doctor he'll know just how much punishment her body can take and she's certain he'll take her to that very limit.

"Please stop, Doctor Shane, please, please PLEASE! It really hurts and I'm so sorry I lied to you, I will never do it again, I promise, I mean it."

"Oh Nurse Ivy, there's much more in store for you. Your punishment has only just begun! I'm going to finish now and you're going to make your 2:00 am rounds. You better hope none of your patients are awake because you're flashing everything you own. No, you can't pull down your skirt. You can try to hide your pussyttttttt, but you can't possibly hide that ripe red bottom!

And your breasts can't be contained in that dress so you better try and cover them with one hand and your pussy with the other. You don't have time to wash your face so you'll just have to go out with it all tear-stained and sticky from cum dripping down your chin.

Nasty liars deserve to be humiliated, but luckily for you it's unlikely anyone will see. Except me witnessing your slutty shame."

"Oh but, Doctor Shane—"

"No, Nurse Ivy. No excuses, no pleading, no arguing just do as you're told. And hurry back for the rest of your spanking."

"WHAT?"

Doctor Shane laughs at her look of shock and horror.

"Oh Nurse Ivy, I'm not nearly done with you. You've still got to take a trip to the examination room with the stirrups, and I'm sure you can figure out what will happen to you there! Don't make me wait a moment longer than necessary, *or else!* Now hurry up."

Hiccuping as she gulps to catch her breath Nurse Ivy opens the door of the Doctor's Lounge and peers out fearfully but there's no one around to witness her shame. She scurries through the ward doing her best to cover up and is deeply relieved that none of her patients has woken.

She doesn't want to go back to Doctor Shane for more punishment but she can't stay out in the open, either. She has no choice and re-enters the lounge with her head hanging down.

Doctor Shane gives her a grin and pats his knee, indicating she needs to get back into position. She draws close but then suddenly her body rebels and she tries to pull back but he's ready for that and grabs her wrist with a grip like steel.

Nurse Ivy stops struggling and when he relaxes his hold she swings her leg around and catches him by surprise. Now, instead of being face-down with her sore bottom trembling in anticipation of more punishment she's straddling him and he grins at her boldness.

She rips her Candy Striper uniform open and pulls it off so now she's kneeling spread-legged over his lap, totally naked. He runs his hands up and down her nude body, enjoying the sight and feel of her.

"I don't need any more spanking, Doctor Shane, I need to be fucked," she pants cupping his hands over her breasts then reaching down to stroke herself. He hefts her tits, feeling the weight of them, and tells her they're a perfect size. Bending his head he takes a hard nipple in his warm mouth and nips at it gently.

Nurse Ivy lets her head fall back, arching her chest towards him, and groaning with pleasure. Her hand rubs faster and he pulls back to watch her masturbate.

"Fuck me!" she demands but he just smiles and shakes his head saying: "Not until I finish spanking you."

"NOOOO! I need you inside me now. Please, Doctor Shane!"

He angles her hips to get a better view of her glistening slit, his eyes narrow as his gaze moves from her face to her rapidly moving hand, his dick getting hard as he enjoys the show she's putting on for him.

"Cum for me naughty girl, show me just how bad you are, be my horny slut."

His dirty talk sends her over the edge and she shatters with a high-pitched yelping sound as she gasps with pleasure. She falls forward, exhausted, into his embrace. Doctor Shane hugs and kisses her before easily turning her over his knee.

Nurse Ivy squeals indignantly but he laughs at her. Then he rubs both full globes for a few moments before lashing down with a quick sharp strokes. Smack! Smack! Smack!

Nurse Ivy is soon sobbing with the pain and begging him to stop.

Doctor Shane begins talking quietly and she has to stifle her moans and cries to hear him. Surprisingly she finds his words soothing.

"I've been waiting for this opportunity for some time, Nurse Ivy. I've known from the moment I met you that you're the type of woman who needs a man with a firm hand. A man who is willing to discipline whenever he deems it necessary. A man who won't back away from a commitment to give you what you want and what you need.

I'm honored to be that man and I will keep you on a tight leash so that you're always secure in the knowledge that I will tend to you and keep you safe. Rest assured that I know what's best for you and I will see that you get it. Often!"

"Doctor Shane, I – oh!, OH!"

"Do you know why I'm giving you this spanking, Nurse Ivy?"

She struggles to speak but finally manages to answer: "Because I lied to you, I lied about the smoking."

"No, that's why I spanked you the first time. The reason you're getting your butt tanned again is because I love doing this! This is my favorite kind of foreplay. You know how men talk about different female body parts? Well I'm definitely an ass man. I love watching how your cheeks sway under your uniform and when you bend over I have to fight the urge to grab your hips and yank you tight against me.

Smacking you rosy red really turns me on. I'll never use a belt or anything that will mark you because I love the look and feel of your smooth blushing skin. You're absolutely beautiful to me like this, squirming and squealing and begging because we both know it's all for show. Oh sure, your bum is stinging but this heat goes deep into your core and you're super turned on.

In fact, I can feel you rubbing your clit against me and I know you're horny again. The endorphins are flowing and you're enjoying the natural release of dopamine into your system with all this sexual activity. Your pain still exists, but it's morphed into pleasure, torment turned into physical arousal. See how your hips are rhythmically humping against me—"

But anything further Doctor Shane might want to say is drowned out by the scream of ecstasy that erupts from Nurse Ivy as she climaxes once again in a heated frenzy. Her very red bottom is dancing in his lap as she finishes with a long drawn-out groan of sated desire.

She falls down limply and he easily lifts her up and around until she's straddled over his lap again and where he can hold her at the waist and tease her wet pussy with his hard cock. Rubbing the head up and down Nurse Ivy's slippery slit he feels her straining to engulf him in her hot sheath.

"Being my girl means indulging me in my favorite foreplay but I'm certain you will come to accept your sessions across my knee with a love/hate attitude when you let the arousal outweigh the sting. If you're willing.."

"Yes, of course I am."

"You are mine, Nurse Ivy, aren't you?"

"Oh God yes, Doctor Shane. Yes! Yes! Yes!"

It's true that she's moved beyond the pain and can only concentrate on her need to ease this ache in her engorged clit and her slick pussy.

"That's my good girl, being a needy greedy slut but only for me."

"Only your hard cock can fill me and satisfy me, Doctor Shane."

He pulls her down hard onto his shaft and powerfully fucks her. Their bodies lock together in sexual intimacy and emotional fulfillment. When she cries out he explodes with her, giving them both the dominance and the submission they crave.

Just what the doctor ordered.

"Wow!" says Derek, "That's really hot stuff, Polly! Please tell me you used to be a Candy Striper?

"If the story starts *Once upon a time* then sure, I can be a Candy Striper in that fairy tale!"

"Have you got our next playtime scripted out yet?" I ask, eager to hear the new story.

"I do, and it's a fun one. It's about a plain Jane virgin with a killer body who gets caught stealing by the handsome security guard.

So when you come home from work on Friday I'll say *Open your bag, Miss* and you'll know you're in trouble big time!"

Thieving Clerk Caught By New Security Guard Setting An Example

Gillian checks her watch and figures she can safely leave now. Old George will have already poured his first cup of coffee and be comfortably settled in his booth at the door.

The store's staff entrance is from the back through the warehouse. Gillian hears the heavy fire-door clang shut behind her and then the only sound is her high heels clicking on the cement floor as she crosses the huge empty space.

Light spills out of the security guard's booth shining a pathway to the exit. Gillian picks up her pace thinking *Five more minutes and I'll be home-free.*

As she approaches the booth she pastes on a smile, knowing she'll need to spend a minute in greeting with the old man, but before she arrives a tall, powerfully-built man steps through the open door.

Gillian comes to an abrupt halt at the sight of this stranger. He'd be a very handsome man if it wasn't for the hard, stern look on his face.

Startled, Gillian stammers: "Wh-where's George?"

Tall, dark and mean silently gives her the once-over before answering in a low gravelly voice: "George has been reassigned to the early morning shift."

"So, who are you?"

He quirks up an eyebrow and again leaves a lengthy pause ahead of his reply: "I'm the new security guard, night watchman shift, and my name is Zoltan."

"Zoltan? That's..."

"Hungarian."

Under his dark, penetrating gaze Gillian's confidence wavers. It suddenly feels like the item hidden in her bag weighs a ton! Struggling to recover her composure she says: "Oh! You're the first Hungarian I've ever met. I'm Gillian Landers and it's nice to meet you, Zoltan."

He reaches out his massive hand and she shifts everything she's carrying - her purse, tote-bag, and car keys – into her left hand so she can shake thinking *Europeans are always so formal in their manners.*

But she's wrong, Zoltan isn't extending a greeting, instead he's saying: "I need to look in your bag, Miss."

His expression hasn't altered a whit but suddenly Gillian knows he suspects her! Does she have a guilty look? Is she sweating? Breathing too fast and too hard?

"I'm not a shopper," she blurts out.

"All bags must be checked," he states impassively.

"I'm the Assistant Manager of Women's Sleepwear and Lingerie!" she announces, pulling herself up straight and staring him in the eye, even though she has to tilt her head back to do so.

He simply repeats his request.

"No! I will not be searched by you, you obviously don't know how things are done around here. You need better training. Old George would never be so insulting—"

Zoltan simply grabs the tote-bag he was reaching for originally.

"Oh how dare you! This is too much and I protest—"

But Gillian's protest dies on her lips when Zoltan pulls the undergarment out of the bag and holds it up between them.

The corset is the sexiest piece of clothing Gillian has ever seen. It's made out of a heavy satin that snugs in the waist tightly when hooked together. The demi-cups push the breasts up high with only lace covering the nipples. The slate blue material, with garter straps in the same color, flares neatly over the hips with only a bit of lace falling over the wearer's vagina while her bottom is fully exposed. It will make her skin look rosy pink, and bring out the blue of her eyes.

She took the matching silk stockings as well.

Zoltan stares at Gillian then tilts his head to indicate he's waiting for an explanation.

"I uh, I bought that."

"Sales receipt?"

"I didn't keep it, this is a non-returnable item." Gillian tries to grab it back but Zoltan simply raises his arm a few inches moving the lingerie beyond her reach.

She hadn't realized just how tall of a man he is, and now she's suddenly struck by how manly and very masculine he is. Coming this close means she can smell his cologne, an unfamiliar but pleasing scent.

"Look give that to me right now, it's mine."

Zoltan finds the price tag still attached and gives a low whistle when he sees how much the corset cost.

"Expensive."

"Not with my Senior Associate's discount. Stop handling it and give it back to me now," Gillian tries to smile adding: "Please, Zoltan."

"A Senior Associate and Assistant Manager who steals."

"It's not stealing, I paid for it, honestly there's an overage in today's sales printout that covers the cost. You can check that with the Manager tomorrow although I hope you won't. See, I can afford it but I can't afford to have anyone know I bought it."

Gillian has quite a plain face but with good skin, and her complexion is now suffused with a bright red blush. She purses her lips and blinks rapidly to fight back the tears that threaten to spill. They make her eyes sparkle but Zoltan isn't interested in her face, not when she's got such a distracting body.

"Why not? Surely you're happy to wear this for your man?"

"That's why not, because I don't have a man."

"Oh, you have a woman instead?"

"A wom.. oh! I see, but no. I have no one, I'm a single woman."

Again she feels his eyes travel up and down her body but his expression doesn't reveal his thoughts.

"Is this a gift to give to another woman?"

"No, it's for me but well... just for me, just to wear when I'm at home on my own. God I sound so pathetic. This is why I don't want anyone to find out!"

"You are the last employee to leave the store tonight."

"I planned it that way."

"Yes, I'm sure you did, a premeditated crime."

"Oh don't be silly. I fully expected Old George to be here and he'd just wave me through."

"Which might be why *Old George* has been re-scheduled. I do not wave anyone through if they're carrying a bag. This is my job and I will do it well. I should make an example of you."

"What? I already told you, I paid for this."

"Even if true, that doesn't matter. You're trying to sneak some merchandise off the premises without a receipt proving purchase."

"But... well, what do you want from me?"

This time when Zoltan eyes her his gaze lingers on her big bust before sliding appreciatively down her torso to wide hips and curved thighs. He turns back to his booth and gestures for her to walk in saying:

"I want you to put this on and show me how it looks."

Shocked, Gillian refuses to budge exclaiming:

"I'm not going to model lingerie for you!"

"Well then I guess I will catch a big fish and make a good name for myself my first day on the job."

"But you can't—"

Folding his muscular arms over his broad chest Zoltan interrupts her saying:

"It's a simple solution."

The way he looms over her is so intimidating and so overwhelmingly macho. He's very domineering. Gillian feels a flutter of some new and unidentifiable feeling – fear? excitement? And nervously fiddles with her hair while thinking about the dilemma she's in. After a moment she asks:

"And if I model this garment for you then you won't report me, is that right?"

"Yes."

"This is just outrageous. It's blackmail, it's extortion, coercion..."

"Yes," he agrees, not in the least bit ashamed of himself.

Why would he be? she thinks bitterly, *I'm the only one who's got reason to be ashamed.*

"Well fine, then. But where can I change? There's no room in that booth."

"No, but it leads into a comfortable, more spacious area."

He gestures again and this time Gillian enters the booth and walks through the door at the back. Zoltan follows with her contraband and after passing it over leans against the door.

"You can't watch me get undressed!" cries Gillian, already embarrassed and angry.

"You're right, I'd rather wait for the great surprise. The unveiling. I'll stand out here with my back to you and you tell me when you're ready for me to turn around."

"I'll never be ready," Gillian mutters under her breath.

"I have excellent hearing," Zoltan replies.

Dismay over her predicament brings the tears back to Gillian's eyes and this time she can't contain them. *I'll be damned if I let him see me cry* she tells herself, roughly brushing them away.

Zoltan hears Gillian sniff and figures out that she's teary, but smirks thinking she'll be sobbing by time he's finished with her.

There's only a very small wall mirror, just big enough to reflect Gillian's face but none of her body in the corset. She tries to recollect how she looked in the change-room but she'd barely had a chance to study the effect, she was so afraid of getting caught. Instead, her plan was to spend a long time studying herself in her mirror at home tonight. Alone.

She never expected anyone to ever see her in the lingerie and now this stranger, this man Zoltan, is going to get an eyeful. Shrugging she decides she might as well go the whole route and slips on the stockings as well then snaps them to the garters. Smoothing the fine silk over her legs she feels beautiful and sexy, although she knows that's just a fantasy.

Her shoes don't match but they have a heel so she steps back into them before telling Zoltan she's ready. Later she will treasure the look on his face when he turns around and catches sight of her.

The only word for Gillian's body is voluptuous. She isn't fat, she's just a full-bodied, well-proportioned woman. The corset might have been designed with her in mind. It flatters her hourglass figure by emphasizing her small waist and showcasing her generous bosom.

She doesn't want to make eye contact, she's so humiliated to be an unloved and lonely old maid standing here like this wearing sexy gear, pretending to be desirable, and feeling so foolish. Zoltan clears his throat and when she looks up he motions for her to turn around.

Gillian is halfway into her spin before she remembers that the back side of the garment ends at her waist. She couldn't bear to wear her plain panties with this marvellous corset so she removed them. Turning will put her completely bare bottom on display. She freezes.

Zoltan steps close, easily moving around for a clear view of her back view. She hears the hiss of his indrawn breath while he murmurs:

"Oh yes, yes. So full and round and smooth. Gorgeous. What a beauty."

Big bottoms are fashionable right now but Gillian has always dressed to minimize hers. Slim, boyish figures were the preferred look when she was a girl so her formative years were filled with insults like *lard ass, thunder thighs,* and *big butt.*

She puts her hands out to cover herself and half-turns back towards him. With her arms pulled back her big breasts are thrust forward and he feasts his eyes.

"This thing, this woman garment is perfect on you. It makes you beautiful and I understand why you took it." He tilts her chin with his big hand until she's looking up in to his eyes. "You are a woman made for something like this but it's still wrong to take it. You didn't follow the rules. And now you want to compromise me into breaking the rules with you."

"Well, as I explained the money is in the till—"

"You know you did wrong, that's why you looked so guilty when I first saw you. You were trembling and that made me suspicious."

Gillian is surprised at how well Zoltan speaks English but she doesn't want to waste time asking him about it. She just wants to get her clothes back on and go home so she can cry in private. To her mind her lovely corset is ruined now that Zoltan has invaded and ridiculed her dream life.

"Wrongdoing should be punished. You need to be punished for what you've done to your employer, and to me - a lowly guard just trying to do his job."

"Punished? What on earth do you—"

Before she can finish her sentence Gillian finds herself lifted and carried over to the desk chair where Zoltan sits down and upends her over his lap.

"Oh no!" she cries, realizing exactly what he has in mind and knowing that the sexy garment leaves her fully exposed.

She tries to cover her behind but Zoltan grabs both wrists in one of his big hands and presses them down against the small of her back. That keeps her from trying to cover herself while anchoring her body across his knee.

His fingers are gentle as they unsnap the garters from the back of the stockings, removing even those frivolous bits of blue lace from his unfettered access to her naked backside.

Gillian hates to hear herself begging but she's desperate, pleading: "No, please don't do this, it's so humiliating! Please, please don't, Zoltan."

His only answer is a resounding smack on her flesh. Gillian has a vague, half-buried memory of seeing her mother pull her younger brother's little corduroy pants down and spanking his bare bottom. He'd broken the snow globe, an ornament he'd been strictly forbidden to play with, and her mother was very angry. After a number of slaps that left the toddler's bottom pink the punishment was over and, surprisingly, the little boy clung to his mother's leg crying loudly *Mommy, Mommy!*

Gillian remembered being disturbed by what she saw and certain she'd never experienced a spanking herself. She's definitely learning a lesson now!

Zoltan quickly follows up the first smack with blow after blow as he does a thorough job. Each stroke he administers stings sharply causing Gillian to flinch and her bum to quiver. She's sure her bottom is turning just as pink as in that memory from decades ago. She feels the heat from his punishing hand spread.

"Your delectable derriere is made for this!" he happily declares.

"You-you-you're enjoying this!" gasps Gillian as she squirms under the increasingly heavy slaps to her already tender bottom.

"Yes, of course! You have a gorgeous bum and I'm laying my mark on it, making it even more appealing the redder it gets. It really is magnificent." He pauses his paddling to squeeze her plump behind, even bestowing kisses.

"You're already very warm but I won't stop until you're very hot!" he promises then continues to fulfill his mission. It's obvious from his attention to detail and his happy mutterings that he's taking a great deal of pleasure in delivering her punishment. Gillian can't understand the words but the murmurs *sound* complimentary.

The heat Gillian feels on her backside is traveling right through her body. The spanking just keeps going on and on until her flesh is on fire. She's making the most embarrassing mewling cries as she begs him to stop but he just chuckles and tells her she has a long ways to go yet.

That makes her kick her legs in a frenzy and after enjoying that spectacle for a while Zoltan hooks his right leg over both of hers. Now she's not only trapped but her bottom is raised up even higher on his left leg giving him access to the sensitive crease between buttocks and thigh. Her sit spot.

He devotes his hand to that tender area and Gillian is soon sobbing with the pain, but her tears don't move him in the least.

Finally he stops but only to announce that he's not done with the spanking yet. He tells her he's noticed that her wriggling made her tits pop out and he wants to spend some time fondling them.

Transferring her wrists to his spanking hand he arches her body back into a bow and grabs a handful of her bare breasts that are bobbing freely.

"Oh yes, yes! You are perfect Gillian. You have a perfect woman's body and it's all mine to play with."

Gillian groans at the shame of it but is relieved her aching bottom is getting some respite. He caresses and fondles her breasts then starts swirling his palm against her nipples. They grow hard while craving a firmer touch. Without realizing it she begins pressing them forward into his hand and he smiles at her response. After a bit more groping he switches her wrists back again and uses his right hand to slip between her legs to explore her private place.

Gillian jerks sharply the moment his fingers touch her. She's never been touched in that spot before. She's holding her breath while concentrating on what he's doing. He's sliding his fingers up and down into her folds, into her slit, marveling out loud at how slick and wet she is.

Gillian squeezes her eyes shut and lets her head drop down, trying to escape this reality, but Zoltan won't leave her in peace. He pushes his finger inside her and groans appreciatively at the tightness he feels there. Gillian feels discomfort and shifts but that only brings her naked pussy in contact with the hard bulge in Zoltan's pants.

"Ah, you feel him, he feels you too! I look forward to showing him to you but first I have some more playing to do right here," and with that he finds her clitoris and begins to mercilessly tease and tweak, tickling one moment and pressing down hard the next. Gillian's pelvis is moving to its own rhythm and she's panting over all the shivery but pleasurable sensations she's newly experiencing.

Now Zoltan's fingers are strumming her clit like a musical instrument and she's gyrating her hips with wanton abandon and moaning loudly. When Gillian climaxes Zoltan is proud and delighted to discover the wildcat he's unleashed and is now determined to tame.

Putting his plans to continue the spanking aside for now he frees his cock and slides Gillian on top of the head. He can feel that she's a virgin so he forces himself to go slow. Inch by inch he lowers her onto his rock-hard shaft and Gillian, after a little gasp at the moment's pain when he breaks through, is soon keening with a hunger she's never known.

Zoltan buries his face in her round breasts and sucks on first one nipple then the other. He so free and easy about giving and taking pleasure without any hesitation, and Gillian's body is made for enthusiastic sex. He's happy to take on the role of teacher and looks forward to introducing her to all of the delights two naked bodies can share.

After her third, or maybe it's the fourth? orgasm, Gillian is spent. Her bones feel like rubber and she lies splayed across Zoltan's body trying to catch her breath. She jumps a bit when his hands cup her sore bottom and squeeze.

"Still hot!" he proudly announces with a big smile. She just shakes her head at him. Already the memory of her pain from the spanking has been steamrollered by all the orgasmic delight from his magical fingers and cock.

Gillian knows she should feel nothing but shame at herself and disdain for this man who treated her so harshly but... her body still vibrates from the delicious ways he has instructed her. She wanted to be his eager and willing pupil and she refuses to pretend otherwise now.

"So, you need to go sleep now, Gillian. You go home and tomorrow you wear this wonderful thing underneath your clothes, yes? and no panties! And when you finish work we will do all this again. And more."

Gillian pulls back to look into his twinkling black eyes in his handsome face. His broad smile makes him drop-dead gorgeous. He's perfectly serious about what he's just told her to do.

"You want to do this again? With me? tomorrow night?"

"Yes, yes, everything. You wear sexy clothes, I spank you red-hot, we fuck. Also, I teach you how to suck my cock, and you learn how to have your pussy licked until you scream with joy."

Gillian is shocked by his crude language but not nearly as much as she is by the rush of heat straight to her very depths. Of course she wants to do this all again tomorrow, even submitting to another shameful but stimulating spanking, but why would this gorgeous man want to do it with her? She really is confused and asks:

"But... why do you want me?"

Now he's the one with a puzzled expression as he says:

"Because now you are my girlfriend," and for the first time their lips meet in a deep, penetrating, dizzying kiss.

"Will you think I'm crazy if I say that's so romantic? I mean, I realize they're strangers and he's coerced her consent – in fact she never did agree to go across his knee – but he turned into such a happy, horny guy as soon as sex was on the table. His carefree attitude swept away all her hang-ups."

"I was inspired by thinking about women who holiday in exotic locales hoping for a vacation fling with a foreigner. No guilt, no strings attached, just mutual pleasure and happy memories."

"In my next scenario you'll be the naughty teenager getting caught and punished by her Daddy's second-in-command."

"Oooh, we're in the Army now!"

Corporal Catches Boss's Naughty Daughter Sneaking In At 2:00 AM

Lulu Carson very slowly slides the glass of her bedroom window until it's open as wide as can be. She pauses, listening hard, but doesn't hear a sound. Nothing, that is, except for her own loud breathing.

But she's home-free, she's done it! She covers her mouth with her hands to stifle the giggle that's triumphant, but also deeply relieved at not getting caught.

Until the overhead light of her bedroom is suddenly switched on and her guilty face is captured in the glare.

Cpl. Gerry Smythe is standing in the doorway, blocking any escape, with his big arms crossed over his massive chest and the meanest, sternest look she's ever seen on his face.

Lulu's father, Calvin "Butch" Carson is a Drill Instructor and Sergeant in the Marine Corps. He excels at mean, stern looks and his corporal has copied him to a T.

Cpl Smythe's laser focus is trained on his superior's errant eighteen-year-old daughter who has just climbed into the house at two in the morning even though she's been grounded for the whole week.

The girl immediately bursts into tears wailing: "Gerry, I can explain!"

Cpl. Gerry Smythe doesn't say anything, he just walks to the window and shuts it. He made some hardware adjustments to it tonight and now latches a padlock and pockets the key. Then he closes the curtains tight. He turns on the bedside table lamp and flips the overhead switch off.

Concern that the neighbors might see or hear what's about to happen in Sarge's daughter's bedroom isn't going to stop him. But he's always liked Lulu so he'd prefer that she not be the subject of gossip. Although the close proximity of Base housing units makes that impossible. In fact, it's unlikely that Lulu's escape and re-entry occurred without being noticed.

Lulu grabs hold of his forearm and tugging hard to get his attention starts complaining that it wasn't fair for her father to ground her and make her miss the concert, that it was her favorite group ever, that everyone was going to be there, and what was the big deal anyway? Here she is home safe and sound and her Daddy need never find out.

Now that she is safely home Cpl. Smythe is able to let the worrisome fear leave his body. He'd imagined all kinds of terrible things happening to Lulu, and when he thought of having to face his Sergeant when he returned from active duty well... Now he can allow the volcanic anger rising inside to build up. He looks down at Lulu's face with her godawful black eye makeup streaked by tears, the pink and purple dyed hair sticking up, her lipstick smeared – and how did that happen? and the unsuitable clothes she's got on.

Lulu is small-busted so she doesn't wear revealing tops but her t-shirt is cropped way too short, showing a lot of naked belly exposed by her Daisy Mae short shorts. For some time now Cpl. Smythe has been disturbed to notice that his superior officer's daughter has a luscious ass.

Through the haze of his anger he imagines all those boys and young men ogling her – maybe even groping and fondling her – in the crowded audience at a rock concert... and with a growl he slips his thumbs in the waistband and yanks hard. He's a very strong young man so when he hears a tearing sound he just pulls harder and is soon ripping the offending article from her body.

Now Lulu is naked from her rib-cage down and he catches a glimpse of red pubic curls before he flips her face down on the bed. Under different circumstances he would love to see Lulu's private parts but this is all about punishment. If exposing her pussy to him has embarrassed her as well then all the better!

While waiting for her he had propped up pillows at the edge of the bed in readiness for her return. He now grabs her by the hips and positions her down with her bare ass pointing skyward.

"I was going to wait until morning and let you cry yourself to bits worrying about it for what remains of this night but then I decided to hell with that, I'll spank you twice. Tomorrow's Sunday so I can give you a good licking in the morning, maybe another in the afternoon, and definitely a bedtime spanking."

"Gerry, nooooo!" cries the girl, sounding about ten years younger than her age.

Cpl. Smythe is unhappy knowing how Sarge's daughter's behavior will deeply shock and disappoint him. Cpl. Smythe was honored when Lulu was entrusted to his care but he never expected something like this. The two of them had actually laughed when Sarge told him if she misbehaved he was to blister her bare bottom with the back of the hairbrush.

Cpl. Smythe and Lulu had always got along well and he thought that once he moves up in rank he'll ask her out. Right now she's forbidden fruit but they are friends. Or at least that's what he thought until she fooled him, and worse, made a fool out of him.

He's angry because he never imagined he'd have to discipline Lulu severely, never expected her to give him cause, but here they are.

"I'm sure the Sergeant never expected I'd be following through on his instructions about how to discipline you if you disobeyed his orders. I'm sorry it's come to this, Lulu."

Despite the fantastic shades of her hairstyle Lulu is a natural redhead and has the milky white skin that matches that coloring. He takes a moment to muse in a detached manner that her ass really is exceptional and turning it fire-engine red is going to release a lot of the pent-up anger and anxiety he felt tonight.

Cpl. Smythe has seen how hard it is on his boss to be the widowed father of a fiery-tempered teenager. If he'd had a son he could easily cow him into submission but his darling girl has him wrapped around her little finger. He told his corporal that he knew he'd been too lenient with her when she sassed him back about the concert and so he grounded her.

Obviously that wasn't enough of a punishment.

"I'm going to spank your ass with this hairbrush until you're screaming from the pain and I'm going to do that every night for the next week because I'm extending your grounding that long. And here's a heads-up: depending on your behavior you might get paddled more than once a day—"

"No! You're not my father, you have no right. I'm an adult now. You're trying to ruin my life!"

Cpl. Smythe continues as if Lulu hasn't interrupted, saying: "You will get a hairbrush spanking every night at bedtime and you can cry yourself to sleep. If you sass me during the day you'll go over my knee for a hard hand-spanking."

"You can't do that!"

Crack! The wooden back of the hairbrush makes a satisfying sound as he brings it down forcefully on her bare bottom. Lulu howls but Cpl. Smythe ignores her and repeats the swatting again and again and again.

"Don't [smack] tell [smack] me [smack] that [smack] I [smack] can't [smack] do [smack] something [smack] when [smack] I'm [smack] already [smack] doing [smack] it [smack] [smack] [smack] [smack]."

"This is abuse!" she sobs.

"You abused my trust," he replies, without pausing the punishment.

He's struck her about twenty times and her flesh is a sore red. She's kicking her legs and thrashing about but he easily holds her in place while continuing to punish her naked backside till it glows.

When he finally stops she screams through her choking cries that she hates him.

His deep voice is a low rumble when he replies: "Well I don't hate you, Lulu. But I sure do hate thinking about your Daddy's heartache at having such a disobedient daughter." And with that he gets up and leaves the room, locking the door.

Cpl. Smythe knows he won't sleep in the master bedroom tonight so he sits in the living-room sipping on a Scotch and thinking about his Sarge and Sarge's dead wife, Maisie, and how differently things would have been if Lulu's mother had been here to raise her.

The Sergeant once told him that although he loves his daughter dearly, Maisie was the love of his life. He's never met – or even seen – another woman who could interest him. Not like his Maisie. Lulu inherited both her red hair and her temper.

Sarge chuckled when he related how there were times when he had to put Maisie across his knee and spank her bare bottom for fighting with him or swearing at him. She was fond of throwing things too. Her paddling sessions always ended up with the two of them in bed in frenzied enjoyment. Something about those sessions really turned them both on.

In fact, there were times when he suspected she'd pick a fight just for the fun of the reconciliation. Well, the fun that came *after* she had her pretty bottom reddened until it looked like a ripe tomato.

Cpl. Gerry Smythe was 100% certain that Sarge never imagined the young man would have to punish Lulu the same way. If so, he sure wouldn't have mentioned the sex afterwards!

But, as Sarge explained, meting out punishment is simply a duty that must be performed to keep an errant, willful girl from going off the rails. Too often the teenaged offspring of Armed Forces parents are overly rebellious so it's vital to keep the rules clear, the discipline firm, and the child safe – no matter what age.

Cpl. Smythe realizes he stopped Lulu's spanking too soon. So long as she could scream out her hatred of him she hadn't learned a damn thing. He considered going back into her room to continue the lesson but decided he'd have plenty of time to make up for his leniency tomorrow.

He dozes for awhile but never falls fully asleep. That's how he knows when his charge has finally cried herself to sleep. By now it's past three am and he settles in the La-Z-Boy for a nap.

Waking up to the sound of church bells he heads to Lulu's bedroom. She is sleeping on her stomach and that's no surprise when he sees her red, swollen behind.

He has a moment of regret but steels his nerve, assuring himself that his only regret is that Lulu disobeyed her father and it's her bad behaviour that has put Cpl. Smythe in this position. He has no need to feel any remorse for carrying out a necessary correction.

He shakes her awake and when she grumbles he drags her out of her bed and onto the floor. She lands on her butt which hurts enough to wake her up instantly and in a bad temper.

"Go to the bathroom," he orders.

"I don't need to go, I just want to sleep."

"Go to the bathroom now or piss your bed – your choice – because I'm locking you in here for the day."

"No! You can't—"

He cuts off her complaint by yanking her to her feet and pushing her out the bedroom door. He hears her go into the bathroom and he sits at the desk waiting impatiently for her return.

"LULU get your ass back in here!" he bellows.

She hurries in with a face like thunder yelling: "I've just seen my bum in the mirror and it's so fucking red and that really is abuse. You've gone too far, Gerry. I'm going to file a complaint—"

But before she gets any further he pulls her across his knee and begins spanking her by hand.

Now she's shrieking as the pain spreads right across her whole backside. Cpl. Smythe's hands are huge and each stroke covers a lot of area, landing vigorously on the same spots, and her bottom - already tender and hot – is now on fire. But he doesn't let up, he won't show any mercy to this foul-mouthed girl this time.

Her behind has a lovely inverted-heart shape – so plump and inviting – encouraging him to deepen the already rich tones he created a few hours ago. He admits to himself that he's enjoying this session with the squirming girl bent across his lap.

"I don't care how sore and red your ass is, Lulu. Every time you step out of line you're getting another spanking until you adjust your attitude. And I will always do a thorough job. Every [spank!] single [spank!] time [spank!] [spank!] [spank!]."

"Stop, please Gerry, Please stop!"

Turning a deaf ear to her pleas he moves his hand around to cover her upper thighs and every single inch of her bottom including the sides right over to her hip bones. Every few strokes he pauses and watches her quiver in anticipation of the next smack and he doesn't disappoint.

After Lulu has received a really hard hand-spanking, she's given a couple of bottles of water to drink, and then she's locked in her room without her laptop or her mobile. She's soon wailing and shouting and pounding on her bedroom door.

He gets into bed and glancing at the clock tells himself what time to wake up. As he settles down to sleep he drifts off to the thought that tonight Lulu will get another session with the hairbrush so he'll probably have to keep her off school tomorrow.

She won't be able to sit down in class with a blisteringly hot bottom, he thinks.

He wonders if Lulu will take after her mother and come to enjoy, or at least be aroused by, her spankings. Something to savor for the future he hopes they might have together. With corporal punishment *by a corporal.*

"You've done it wrong Derek, because there's no sex! It's just a straight punishment spanking. That's no fun."

"You're right. Let's see, umm, how about if Lulu, who knows that Smythe has feelings for her, seduces him into not spanking her again?"

"Oh yes, he's a young man so she can probably get out of the next spanking easily. She'll just have to be down on her knees waiting for him when he unlocks her bedroom door."

"Okay, let's try that out. How about this:

At 23:00 hours on Sunday Cpl Smythe comes to Lulu's bedroom to give her the promised bedtime spanking with the hairbrush. As he enters the room he sees her kneeling, completely naked, in the middle of the room.

Surprised at the sight of her nude body his first thought is that her breasts might be small but they're perfectly shaped and his stirring cock has noticed that her little nipples are hard and red.

"Lulu!" he admonishes, "What do you think you're doing?"

"I don't *think* anything Gerry, I *know* exactly what I'm doing. I'm offering you a blow job that will bring you to your knees. Come here and let me swallow you up."

"Stop it right now. That's disgusting talk and... oh I get it. You're just trying to distract me from giving you your spanking. Well Lulu that ain't gonna work, uh-uh little girl. You're going to get that spanking and because of this slutty behavior of yours it's going to be even harder than I'd originally planned on. So up you get."

He pulls her up but her arms snake around his neck and she presses her bare body against him. He can feel the hard points of her nipples through his t-shirt. It's sexy for her to be totally naked while he's fully dressed. She wraps one leg over his hip and draws his groin tight into her and then she starts wiggling against his cock.

He's instantly hard when she licks his ear and whispers: "Gerry I'm so wet for you."

He's a healthy young man who doesn't have a steady girlfriend... it feels like his cock will explode.

Before he can utter a word her mouth has found his and suddenly he's kissing her back. Deep kissing, their tongues twining, she's breathing heavily into his mouth and her hands are running over his shoulders, up and down his back. Now she's grinding her mound into his hard-on while turning him round and dragging him down on her bed.

Instead of lying face-down waiting to be punished she's on her back with her legs spread wide and her wet clit peeking through red curls.

"Do I have to beg, Gerry? I will if that's what you want."

"Lulu, stop!"

"Please fuck me, Gerry. Don't you like my pretty snatch? Please, please I need to feel you inside me filling my hole, making my legs shake when you shatter me, I want you so much. Oh God Gerry, pleeeeeease!"

Bending her knees she lifts up her pelvis in invitation and Cpl Smythe can't resist the temptation of that sweet pink slit beckoning him inside. He knows Lulu is off-limits but he cannot resist her summoning. Breaking the rules adds an edge of extra excitement. Dropping his pants he drives deeply into her welcoming and wet cunt and fucks her again and again and again.

Neither of them gets much sleep that night. It seems each time one of them rolls over in bed the other awakens instantly, already primed and aroused. Gerry tells her he'll call the school in the morning to book her off for the week but Lulu says no, just for Monday. She'll go back on Tuesday as usual.

"How? You didn't get spanked last night but you're going to get your punishment tonight and I don't want you going to school and talking about it until it's all over."

"I have no intention of being punished again Gerry, not by you or anyone else," Lulu comments coolly. "And before you say anything let me remind you that you fucked me all night and you'll be in way more trouble with Daddy then I am *if I tell him*."

"Blackmail, Lulu?"

"Well don't you military guys have a name for it... mutual assured destruction? or something like that?"

"Hmm, your father won't like to hear I've fucked you but neither will he like hearing you instigated it."

"Who do you think he's going to believe? The horny young guy taking advantage or his innocent little girl?"

Gerry moves so fast Lulu doesn't realize what's happened until she's back across his knee with his right leg securing both of hers firmly in place. She can't free herself from the strong hold of his muscular legs. Her groin can even feel the hardness of the muscles in his thighs. He's back in Cpl Smythe mode and about to let her know he's got the upper hand... about to let her *feel* it too!

First he smooths his palm in circles over her plump flesh, then he squeezes and caresses, making sure he fondles both full globes. He can see her trembling in anticipation so he decides to draw the torment out.

"You know what's coming, don't you baby?" he croons.

"Fuck off, Gerry!" she shouts with defiance, but he only chuckles saying: "Mmm-hmm, this is a fine ass, Lulu. It's designed to feel the weight of a man's hand on it. My hand."

He strikes hard and she flinches.

"I love to see you wearing my hand-print, baby." He smacks again and makes sure to strike her hard enough to smart.

"Gerry!" she wails, trying to reach back to cover herself.

"Uh-uh, no hiding this gorgeous derriere." With his left hand he holds both of her wrists together behind her back. Now he's rubbing her rear-end and asking if she's ready for a good hard spanking of the two to three dozen smacks that she's earned.

Frantic at the thought of such punishment on her already-sore bottom Lulu begs and pleads: "Please Gerry, no!"

"*Please* and *No*? Is that all you've got to say? Don't you want to tell me to *fuck off* again?"

He applies a dozen rapid hard strokes. Lulu is squealing and gasping with the pain while trying to kick her legs but they're trapped.

"Want to make a deal, Lulu?"

She doesn't answer so he adds another dozen painful smacks.

"What? Yes, okay."

Now she's teary and writhing, overcome by the scorching of her sensitive skin. He slips his finger in her slit and finding her swollen clit starts giving her different strokes.

"Each night you can be fucked or spanked, your choice." His finger circles the hard little nub and roughly fiddles with it. Lulu can't prevent a groan escaping her lips. Now she's squirming against his finger, trying to get herself off.

He gives her half-a-dozen sharp slaps saying: "Never mind playing, answer me."

"Yes Gerry, of course. I would love to be fucked by you every night until Daddy gets home and it will be our little secret."

"Fucked and sucked."

Silence from Lulu until another dozen swats hit hard.

"Yes, okay! Okay! I'll suck your dick too."

"And I'll suck you until you're a whimpering mess. Would you like me to stop spanking and start licking now?"

"Oh yes, Gerry. Yes, I'd really like that."

"I lost count but I think you got about three dozen swats. Of course the actual number doesn't matter, what does is achieving a deep red color and creating a compliant and obedient girl."

Feeling her stiffen at his remarks he laughs out loud saying: "Oh Lulu, you're your own worst enemy!" before continuing the spanking with at least two dozen more punishing smacks.

By the time he's finished Lulu is his perfect little submissive with a tear-stained face and burning bottom and, most importantly of all, a very wet and willing pussy eager to welcome him in.

He lifts her onto the bed and draws her legs over his shoulders. Her pussy is inches from his mouth and at the mercy of his tongue. He brings her to the edge of orgasm then backs off, then does it again. He smiles to himself thinking that Lulu might be a tease but he's a master of torment. He really enjoys this game of edging and he plays her some more.

Soon she's crying out louder than she did when he spanked her.

He brings her to orgasm several times before burying his shaft deep in her tight wetness. She cums again while he fucks her hard. Afterwards he lays back and pulls her to lie on top of him. His hand cups her ass and he chuckles to feel the heat of her flesh.

"Lulu, the night before Sarge gets home I am going to have to spank you again. You know damn well the neighbors will say something about your escapade on Saturday night so you're going to have to present him with the evidence of a red-hot bottom or else he'll be the one wielding the hairbrush - and you sure don't want that to happen!"

Lulu snuggles closer and says "Whatever you want, Gerry," thinking she can endure one more hard spanking if it means five more nights of sharing her bed with him. Her Daddy is a tough act to follow but she's found a man who has earned her respect... and one she can count on to correct her disobedience when she deliberately provokes him!

"Oh much, much better Derek! I love the idea of Lulu working her womanly wiles to turn spanking time into screwing time. When we act it out I'll definitely have fun using my womanly wiles on you!"

"Mmm, well then maybe you should start practising right now."

*****

Two weeks later, a couple of days ahead of our Special Friday, Derek announces:

"It's your turn to devise our next playtime script, Polly."

"I know and I've got a cute idea. It's about a college freshman and the Big Man on Campus and her pledging task during sorority rush week..."

College Sorority Pledge's Embarrassing Hazing

"Oh no, oh no, oh no-no-no-no-no I CAN'T DO THIS!!!" Jenna cries out.

Becky and Tina hurry over to read the hazing assignment Jenna has received on her phone.

"OmiEFFINGgod!" gasps Becky.

"Oh no Jenna, that really sucks!" agrees Tina.

Several of the cheerleaders are huddling over someone's cell-phone and when Jenna looks across the playing field at them they laugh and point at her.

Belle is the worst and Jenna is suddenly certain this final task for her initiation is 100% Belle Marsden's idea. Just because Chris smiled and said hello yesterday...

Walking across the Quad Jenna, Becky, and Tina had to pass by a group of Frat Boys who whistled and catcalled the *newbies*. The three girls ignored them but then one deep voice called out a pleasant:

"Helloooo, Jenna. Lookin' good!"

And it was Chris Palliser of all people!

"How does the Captain of the Football team know your name, girl?" squealed Becky, and Jenna had to admit she has no idea.

"Well, somebody's not too happy about it," stated Tina with a nod of her head towards Belle and her cohorts who were standing nearby and looked at the three younger girls with angry eyes and pursed up mouths.

That was yesterday and now Belle has sent Jenna a pledging challenge that's impossible to complete. So much for joining the number one sorority here.

Jenna, Becky, and Tina have accepted and completed all their humiliating tasks leading up to today's final assignment. They've been made to look foolish with Jenna having to wear heavy make-up on one eye only all day, and that included one false eyelash. Becky had to come to class in curlers and face cream, while Tina had to stumble around without her glasses. All three girls had had to wear pyjamas to the Student Bar on Friday night.

Everyone knows they're pledging and pokes good-natured fun at them as well as the rest of the new students wanting to join a fraternity or sorority for their college years. It's a well-known rite of passage.

But this task is beyond humiliating. It's... it's diabolical.

"This is so damn unfair!" exclaims Becky.

"Yeah, isn't there someone else we can talk to? Like the president or any of the top girls? This is pure spite," adds Tina.

"That's right. You've done all the stupid stuff they made you do, it isn't right to give you a ridiculous task like this in order to finish."

"No, I can't go complain to anyone because word will get out and then I look like a whiner. If they really wanted me in the sorority they wouldn't make me do something like this... so I guess that's my answer."

"No, that's not right! It's only Belle and it's only because she dated Chris Palliser a few times. Obviously he just wasn't into her or they'd still be together. She shouldn't be allowed to take it out on you."

"Yeah, Jenna. Belle shouldn't win."

Jenna looked between her two friends and hated to see their pity. An unaccustomed resolve rose within her and she straightened her shoulders declaring: "Fuck it, I'm gonna do it!"

"WHAT!!!" her friends shriek in unison.

"Yeah, I'm going to. If Chris blows me off then so what – I've had a moment's embarrassment and—-"

"But it won't be a moment. It will haunt you for the rest of your time here. If Chris doesn't spread the tale Belle certainly will."

"No, I don't think so. It will look bad on her to have given a new pledge such a difficult task that just happens to involve her ex-boyfriend, don't you think?"

"She's got a point," Becky says to Tina.

"Well sure, but neither of you is considering the even worse-case scenario: what if he says *yes?*"

Jenna gulps in surprise. She hasn't really thought this through. What if he does say yes? She'll have to go through with it and Belle will know because the assignment will only be complete when Chris says so.

What will Belle say about her then?

"You know, I think the same argument applies. I think Belle would come out of this looking worse than me."

"Yes, but if he says yes then, omigod Jenna!"

"No wait! Maybe you can reason with him," says Tina all excited with an idea. "Show him your task on your phone, he'll see it comes from

Belle, and ask if he won't play along and pretend. Just to get back at her, like."

"Do you know, I think that might work," muses Jenna. She re-reads the text she received:

Belle: Your final task for admission to our sorority is to tell Chris Palliser that you are a naughty girl who needs to be put across his knee for a sound spanking on your bare bum. Chris must confirm by midnight tonight that you have made the request, and by midnight tomorrow that he has done the job.

"Great idea Tina, no wonder you're the brains of this bunch. What will you do if he refuses, though?"

"Then I'll be back where I started, I guess. What the hell, I'm going to accept this challenge before I can change my mind."

Her friends gasp in delighted horror as Jenna types in her acceptance and hits Send.

Looking across at the clutch of girls waiting for the text to come in they see them smile and applaud. All except Belle who looks really pissed off. A moment later another text arrives with a ding!

Belle: You can't tell him this is a pledge task or show him this text.

"Oh as if! She should have thought about that sooner," says Jenna showing her phone to her friends.

"That's right, she can't change the rules after you accept the challenge."

"Text back right now and say so."

Jenna's fingers fly over the keypad.

Jenna: I've already accepted so the rules of the challenge can't be changed now.

"Whatever you do don't lose that message thread!" warns Tina.

"God, you're right. I'm going to forward it to each of you as back-up."

Just then, Janine, a member of the sorority walks over to them saying she and some of the others think this request of Belle's is outrageous, and if Jenna feels she has to back out they are willing to argue her case and suggest another task.

"Thanks! that's so nice of you, Janine. See this is why we want to pledge, because this sorority has the best membership, really great people."

"Well, I know you've accepted the challenge but if you change your mind, or run into difficulties, just let me know."

As the older girl walks away Jenna's determination to beat Belle at her own game strengthens. She will do this, she'll talk Chris into going along with her plan, and she'll come out on top over her rival.

"Football practice is over," comments Becky looking out across at the players who have finished their workout.

"No time like the present, I guess," says Jenna.

"Good luck!" says Tina, while Becky echoes the sentiment saying: "You go, girl!"

Before Chris Palliser can disappear into the building with the change-rooms Jenna hurries across the field to intercept him. As usual he's got several friends hanging around but when he sees her heading his way he stops and waits.

Jenna is certain her face is bright red as she asks, stumbling over her words:

"Chris, uh.. can I, um.. speak to you? Just, just for a minute. If that's okay?"

He's a big guy made huge by the padded football gear he's wearing. Jenna suddenly feels very small and shy but the blond giant smiles and says:

"Sure! but Jenna I stink right now, I've got to have a shower before I'm presentable."

It's a hot, sunny day and the team has been working out for about an hour wearing their full equipment so Jenna understands but is frustrated at having to wait. She's worrying that she'll have trouble keeping up her nerve, but she can't very well push the man when she's asking for a favor.

It's not just worry that's making her anxious, it's a very real feeling of trepidation because in the last few minutes she's become forcefully aware that Chris Palliser is a man. Up till now she's dated boys her own age but Chris is a couple of years older and already a grown man.

Pondering over the effect this realization is having on her Jenna doesn't hear Chris approach until he's right beside her. Obviously he's rushed to get ready since his fair hair is still wet from his shower.

He's wearing a lightweight v-neck sweater with jeans and even without the protective sports equipment he stands tall and wide. Chris has broad shoulders and a solid body with muscular arms and thighs. The sleeves of his sweater are pushed up over his forearms, the blond hair there glinting in the light. His arms look very strong, and his hands look huge.

Now that he's here, ready to listen, and the two of them are alone Jenna is finding is very hard to begin. Just then a couple of Chris's team-mates come out of the building and head towards him but he waves them off while suggesting he and Jenna take a walk.

He guides her by the elbow and she decides she has to just plunge right in, it's easier to talk without actually looking at him. As they walk side-by-side she keeps her eyes on their shadows and figures out that they're heading east, going towards the parking-lot.

"Chris we haven't actually met which is partly why this is so difficult... but I want to ask you for a favor that's part of my pledge initiation?" she hears her voice go up like she's asking a question and taking a deep breath tries to sound more confident.

"I'm asking because it involves you. Here, read this text," she says thrusting her phone at him. The dainty mobile looks so small in his big hands.

"I can't read it in this light," he states and looking around finds a sheltered spot under some trees. There's a picnic table there so the two of them walk over and sit down.

Jenna is nervously twisting a long strand of hair around her fingers while she waits for him to read the message.

"Can I keep reading the rest of the thread?" he asks and she nods, impressed by his respectful courtesy.

Again she waits until he finishes, and when he does he looks into her eyes with a question in his.

"I'm so sorry you've been put on the spot like this," Jenna rushes to explain. "I was thinking maybe we could say I asked, and then both pretend and say it happened, and then you'd be off the hook. Me too."

"Hmm. I hear what you're saying and yeah, that is a plan but... I'm not comfortable lying about a pledge. I have good standing in my fraternity and if it ever got out well, it wouldn't be good, it wouldn't be right."

Jenna bites down on her lip to keep it from trembling as she feels the threat of tears. She really had hoped to convince Chris to help her out and get back at Belle, too. But maybe he wants to get back *with* Belle, not *at* her. For some reason she finds that thought distasteful.

"I understand. After all, you don't know me and here I am asking for favors. It seems I've upset your ex-girlfriend or maybe not an ex anymore—"

"Very definitely an ex," interrupts Chris.

"Oh!" smiles Jenna, before recalling herself to the task in hand. "Actually, Janine - do you know her? She's a sorority sister and she told me a few of them felt this wasn't right and would back me if I wanted to ask for a different challenge, or a challenge from someone else..."

"So you have a solution already?"

"Well, yes and no. I mean, Janine very kindly offered but if I go that route it will definitely cause friction in the sorority. People will feel the need to take sides and you know I think I'd win, but it's a case of *at what cost?* Do you know what I mean?"

He rests a hand on Jenna's shoulder and she tilts her face up to look in his eyes. Chris is smiling down at her and she's conscious of how close together they are. His lips are only inches away...

Chris gives her a light kiss on the mouth then pulls back saying: "I think you're a very nice girl, Jenna. With good principles. You didn't complain when I said I don't feel right about telling a lie so I think that means you're not big on lying either."

"No, I hate it. Well, I'm no good at it for starters..."

"I thought paddling was a fairly common hazing tradition among the sororities?"

"It used to be, but I guess people felt it was too embarrassing or violent or triggering or something. And of course that was just girls with girls not.. well, a...a man."

He smiles at that then says: "You know, there is another way to solve this dilemma without involving the sorority house in a cat-fight."

"What's that?" Jenna asks.

"We could just do it."

"Just do... you mean, you, um you would, uh..." her voice trails off uncertainly.

"I mean that you could say the words you're supposed to say, and I will agree, and then we'll arrange a time and place to do the deed. That way both of us will have honorably fulfilled our obligations to the letter."

"So you're saying you would agree to... to this?" she waves her phone at him.

"Jenna, it would be my honor to help you." His hand moves down to cover hers which he squeezes and now his arm is across her shoulders. "Just say the words so I can confirm that you asked."

"Oh boy, this is... this is really embarrassing, you know?"

"I kind of think that's the point," he says with a smile while his eyes twinkle at her. Jenna is entranced and hesitates a moment too long before replying: "It is, yeah. Okay here goes nothing."

She keeps her eyes on her phone while she reads out the proper words: "Chris Palliser I'm a naughty girl who.. who needs to be put across your knee for a, oh God, for a sound spanking on my bare... bum. Please."

She didn't think her cheeks could burn any redder but she feels the blush heat up even more.

There's silence between them and when it goes on too long Jenna looks up to find Chris's eyes are still twinkling but with interest as well as amusement as he answers: "It will be my pleasure!"

Jenna knows her face is flooded with color and she ducks her head down but Chris reaches out a finger to stroke her rosy cheeks saying, "Hmm, I guess this is a preview of what I can expect to see when..."

Now Jenna closes her eyes at the shame of it all but he pulls her close and his mouth finds hers in a warm kiss, his tongue gently exploring. She feels herself melt into his embrace and he tightens his grip.

Pulling back he brushes her hair back off her face. His skin around his eyes is crinkled with laugh lines and Jenna is filled with wonder that this very handsome and attractive man has his arms about her at this very moment. And he's willing to... well, to help her.

She can't believe he's actually agreed to do this and then the realization hits her: that she's about to get a spanking on her bare bottom by the Captain of the Football team, the most popular guy on campus. Who she's only just met... and she *asked* for it!

Omigod, she thinks, *it will be so embarrassing! me bent over his knee with my panties pulled down and him... omigod!!!*

"I always say *no time like the present* so let's make some plans."

"I say that too! In fact, I just said it to my girlfriends and then I came over to talk to you."

"You wanted to get it over with. That makes sense. There's no denying this is all a bit awkward, right?"

"Yes, and oh I'm so glad you see it that way too."

"Okay let's you and I go have a couple of drinks to relax and then we'll go back to my room and I'll make sure we're nice and private for your... session. What do you think?"

"Wh-what now? You mean do this thing now?"

"Sure. Unless you'd like to stew over it all night long wondering and waiting until tomorrow?"

"Oh God no, um sure, you're right let's get it over with. I could really use a drink."

"Good girl. I think we'll avoid the Student Bar, too many people will try to poke their noses in our business, so let's go to the lounge at the Colonial Hotel. It's close by and I doubt if we'll run into many – if any – fellow students there."

Before she can question the plan Chris stands and leads Jenna from the field to the parking-lot and his bright blue sportscar.

It only takes them ten minutes to get to the hotel but once they arrive Chris suddenly thinks to ask Jenna if she's twenty-one and she realizes that she can't go into the lounge because she's only nineteen. She's a young-looking nineteen and always gets carded.

"Oh no, I'm sorry Chris. I never thought! Getting served at the Student Bar has never been a problem."

"No, that's because it's licenced as a private club by the school. But it's no problem, sweetheart, what do you drink? We can swing by the liquor store and I can pick up whatever you like."

"Actually, I don't know if you toke I mean, being on the football team and all, but I do have a couple of joints on me."

"That's an excellent idea. We'll have to smoke in the car, I can get expelled if I'm caught with drugs in my room, but we'll drive back and park first, then we can partake."

"Oh I'm glad you're okay with it because I really, really do need to try and relax."

"Awww, baby, don't worry. I'll take care of you. Meanwhile we'll listen to some soothing music, too." Chris pushes in a CD, telling Jenna that he can't get a media player that will work with his classic car. "And here's a classic album to listen to."

A mellow voice sings the golden oldie *"Let's Get It On"*.

"Oh I like this song. Where do you get the CDs?"

"I order online, but now that most of my friends are streaming all their music they're passing their CDs on to me, rather than just tossing them out. I've built up quite a collection."

They park in Chris's assigned spot at the frat house where he lives. Jenna produces the joints but they only smoke one before both agree that they feel ready to get the job done.

She follows him into the house and up the stairs, keeping her head down so she doesn't have to make eye contact with anyone. Splitting a joint has helped but she's still very nervous and once inside Chris's room she suddenly feels incredibly shy and embarrassed.

"Don't worry, Jenna. No one would ever think to come barging in here. I'll lock the door anyhow, and I'll put on some loud music so no one can hear anything, but actually this old house is really solid, I mean look at the thickness of the door, so we'll be fine."

Feeling reassured by his consideration Jenna lifts her face up and looks around the room. It's basically just a bed, a desk, and a chest of drawers. Much like her room in the dorm. Chris has selected something heavy metal, a loud instrumental, to block sound.

But she can hear him clearly enough when he sits on the bed and extends his hand towards her saying:

"Come here, you naughty little girl. It's time for your spanking."

His proximity, their privacy, and the words he's just spoken combine to send a thrill of desire through Jenna's body. She's struck by the realization that Chris Palliser is about to see her semi-naked, and she finds she really likes the idea. The weed has definitely kicked in.

She doesn't realize that her request has played right into his fantasies. Added to that is the fact that he's delighted to be with her, a girl he noticed the moment she set foot on campus.

She comes closer and lets him pull her across his lap. His thighs are hard beneath her pelvis and he holds her easily in the proper position. Jenna is wearing an a-line dress which hangs loosely so he takes hold of the hem and draws it up to her waist. She knows she put on panties this morning, because she doesn't wear a thong with a dress, but she can't remember which ones and if they're pretty or not. It doesn't matter, he's already pulled them down!

She can hear his breathing as he studies the sight before him. He gently caresses first one mound of buttock then the other. Jenna feels her body tremble in anticipation, she has no idea how enticing she looks.

"Great ass," he tells her. "Now for the *sound spanking* as requested!"

Neither Jenna's parents nor grandparents have ever lifted a hand to her so she has no idea what to expect from a spanking – other than what she's seen in movies or read about in books. She's completely unprepared for the reality: it really hurts!

Chris takes his duty seriously by spanking her in a steady rhythm with each smack stinging as he slaps his hand down again and again and again. She soon feels the heat of this paddling and it's a heat that seeps right into her very being. His big hands are covering every inch of her tender young behind.

Unawares, she's begun writhing and wiggling in a futile attempt to escape that relentless hand and as she shimmys she's stimulating her clit against the hard-on in his jeans. Excitement floods through her body and all of her wriggling has really turned Chris on as well.

As she feels his palm bouncing off her reddening flesh her hips are moving in sync. He increases the tempo and force of each smack making Jenna give out little gasping squeals of pain at the burning sensation, and moans of arousal from her core.

What a spectacle she's making of herself! She realizes tears are streaming down her face and knows they're caused by the humiliation she's experiencing as much as the stinging pain. She feels like she's a sex slave or something but thinking about how she willingly submitted to Chris's authority is super hot.

After what seems like forever Chris stops spanking and starts gently fondling and caressing the flesh he's scorched. Jenna finds his soft touch soothing.

"I think this qualifies as a *sound spanking* Jenna because you poor bottom is very red and looks so sore. I think I got a bit carried away and I'm sorry for that, but it's a real turn-on having you across my knee like this. Does it make you horny, too?"

Jenna is awfully glad she's face down right now because she knows her blush is back in full force.

"I think that yes, maybe a little, I guess..." her voice trails away as she feels his fingers slip between her hot butt cheeks and slide into her wet pussy.

The sucking sound his stroking fingers make intensifies her shame but she can't help but let her legs fall open to improve his access to her sensitive spot. He gives a groan of pleasure and his breathing quickens.

Chris pulls the dress up and over her head then quickly unhooks her bra. Jenna reaches to pull it down her arms and now she's completely naked in his lap although he's still fully dressed.

Chris turns her over, cradling her in his strong embrace. He enjoys having her naked in his arms and she loves feeling wanton and desirable.

Pulling back so he can look at her breasts, he kisses and then pinches her hard nipples. He massages and squeezes enjoying the soft warmth of her firm, round tits. Jenna arches her back and pulls her legs even wider apart which makes him chuckle as he returns his attention to her clit.

She wriggles under his touch, making mewling sounds of want and need. After he brings her to climax she tugs up his sweatshirt and presses her breasts against his chest, sharing the feeling of warm skin on skin.

Her own flesh is so soft yet firm, supple and toned, and her nipples are hard little points rubbing across his chest hair. He strips in a matter of moments, proud of his athlete's body.

It's natural that they slide into position with Jenna straddling Chris's lap so his freed cock can find its way inside her wet pussy. They rock in unison with him lifting her up and down the length of his shaft, kissing her breasts and cupping her warm bottom.

It doesn't take long for the two young people to climax together, and the resiliency of their youth quickly readies them for round two. This time they stretch out on Chris's bed and enjoy a more leisurely pace, prolonging their pleasure.

Afterwards she licks him clean, gently lifting his sack so her tongue can reach all around his balls. He's already hard again when he scoots down to return the favor. Chris holds off on his own orgasm until his tongue has teased her into a wriggling mess of desire. This time their coupling is fast and frantic and so fulfilling.

Jenna is filled with wonder curled into Chris's body and feeling the security of his strong and sweaty embrace. He caresses his little girl so gently. She's so delicate and petite but she's taken everything he's given her without complaint.

Soon their passionate kisses escalate them into a driving, craving lust to crash into each other and stay locked together once again in that age-old desire to be one. Finally exhausted their bodies break apart from each other, but they keep holding hands.

Chris props himself up and rummages around their discarded clothing to find his phone in his jeans pocket.

"I'd better send off this text now in case we fall asleep or something," he says. Bringing up Belle's number from his Contacts list he sends her a message writing:

Chris: done and done lotsa fun xxx

"That'll drive her crazy," he says with a satisfied smile.

Jenna sits up with a gasp exclaiming: "Oh! I've completed all my tasks so they've got to make me a sorority sister now!"

"Little girl, with the boyfriend you've got, Captain of the Football Team and all, there was never any doubt that you'd get in."

"Boyfriend?" said Jenna hopefully.

"Well I guess! I mean, you're not going let just anyone put you across their knee and bare that gorgeous ass for a sound spanking when you've been naughty, are you?"

"You've got a great imagination when it comes to horny college kids, Polly. This will be extra fun because I'll love seeing you play the blushing teenager!"

"And you are definitely the kind of man who will just sit back and smile, enjoying every minute of the girl fumbling her way through embarrassing requests and explanations!"

*****

Derek has been spending a lot of time on the books for his new client, a Condo Corporation, so I'm sure that's what inspired his latest scenario. I told him there better not be any naked nubile tenants when he presents his Auditor's Report at their AGM!

Condo Board Prez has to Discipline Nude Sunbathing Homeowner

"Listen, Pops. You deal with the old biddy making the complaint and I'll deal with the hottie who can't keep her clothes on, okay?" says Josh.

tHis father gives him a grateful look explaining that although Miss Kirkley will do her best to bully him at least he's not frightened of her, not like that Miss Conklin.

"As President of the Condo Board you're volunteering your free time and you don't need a hassle from these women fighting and causing trouble. You tell the old prude to stop looking if she doesn't want to see her neighbor sunbathing, and I'll tell the sunbather to be sure to keep her clothes on."

"Well if you're sure you don't mind doing this, Joshua. Miss Conklin is probably a very nice young lady but the thought of her nude is... too unsettling." replies the older man.

In agreement over this plan the father and son head out to the different townhouses to discuss the complaint and possible remedies.

Josh rings the doorbell at Number Fourteen but there's no answer. He figures the homeowner is still in her backyard so he hammers on the door with his fist. Peering through the door's decorative glass panel he sees a figure marching down the hall towards him. The door is flung wide and a gorgeous blonde looking very pissed off glares up at him.

She has to look up because he's over 6 feet tall, towering more than a foot above her. Despite her small stature she carries her voluptuous body well, even if she's having trouble keeping it covered. The towel she's clutching is fighting a losing battle and that's caught his interest so he steps forward, forcing her to step back, and now he's inside her home.

Lucy is entranced by the handsome man staring at her, his eyes filled with admiration and giving her such an intense look. She's very much aware of her nudity as he eyes her up and down, with his gaze feeling like hands crawling and caressing all over her. He gives her a happy smile which makes her smile back but then his grin turns wolfish and Lucy feels her stomach flip. He's such a hunk!

She steps back again but he comes closer, crowding her, his strong muscular body overwhelming her. She feels so petite and feminine in comparison.

"There's been a complaint," he announces.

"Who are you?" she demands.

"I'm with the Condo Board and we've received a complaint, about goings-on in this unit, so we need to investigate."

"Goings-on? What do you mean?"

"Perhaps we could sit down Miss Conklin, to discuss the issue in detail?"

"That's *Ms Conklin* and you've come at a very inconvenient time – I'm not even dressed!"

"And that introduces the subject of the complaint, namely your nude and lewd behavior."

"My WHAT behavior? shrieks Ms Conklin, "Who's making accusations?"

"As I said, if we could sit down? By the way my name is Josh, Joshua Reardon."

Josh has been inching forward through the conversation and Ms Conklin is feeling intimidated by his encroachment into her personal space. She's backed into the living-room but she really doesn't want to go any further until she can get some clothes on, even if he is drop-dead gorgeous.

"Please stop!" she demands, holding up her hand. "I don't know you, you're in my home, you're making these wild claims, and I'm not prepared for a visitor just now."

Josh tilts his head and gives her a devastating smile. Now, completely flustered by his attention, attraction, and proximity Ms Conklin loses her cool. Stomping her foot she angrily yells at him to leave her alone, to get out, and to fuck off.

Without understanding how things happened so quickly Ms Conklin finds herself face down across Josh Reardon's knee with the inadequate towel pulled off and her naked body exposed and helpless. Before she can utter a word of indignant protest his heavy hand smacks down on her bare bottom and he proceeds to give her a good old-fashioned spanking.

In an unhurried and perfectly conversational tone Josh explains:

"I don't appreciate you using that kind of language towards me, Ms Conklin, it is completely uncalled-for. I'm volunteering my time to help maintain harmony in this condo community and I don't deserve your disrespect."

"And just what do you call this behavior, hmm? You are disrespecting me in the worst possible way. I'm naked! You're a stranger! This is my home and I'll use whatever language I want! You come barging in and start assaulting me—"

Josh interrupts her tirade, but without pausing her correction as he does so:

"This isn't assault, it's a well-deserved spanking for your bad attitude. Probably long overdue, in fact... have you ever had your bottom spanked Ms Conklin? On the bare, or otherwise?"

"Of course not! And stop what you're doing RIGHT NOW!"

"Ahhh, that explains a lot. You're too independent and too outspoken. And foul-mouthed with it. If you'd been put across your Daddy's knee often, you would have learned proper manners long before now. But the good news is *it's never too late.* Some good strong discipline will soon set you straight."

All this while Josh's hand has been firmly applying stroke after stroke until Ms Conklin's pretty behind has turned quite a deep pink. Now she's wiggling and crying out with each stinging smack, begging Josh to stop, and even offering apologies for swearing at him.

He decides to ignore her pleas for a little longer because he's enjoying himself too much to stop too soon!

Once he's satisfied his little lesson has had an impact he does stop, telling her that her apology is accepted. He then begins lightly massaging her plump derriere, enjoying the warmth and admiring the view. Ms Conklin has a sweet round bottom, generous hips and thighs thick enough to embrace a man when his shaft is plunged deep inside her.

The little moan of pleasure that escapes Ms Conklin's lips brings a smile to Josh. During the spanking he'd suspected that some of her squirming wasn't to escape his punishing hand but to rub her clit against the bulge in his jeans. He slips a finger down between her warm cheeks and it slides through wet folds of tender flesh. She wriggles against his hand but once she realizes what she's doing she forces herself to stop moving.

Miss Conklin is torn between warring emotions. Her mind is appalled, ashamed, and angry at his cavalier treatment. A spanking for godssake! The archaic practice of a domineering patriarch. Unfortunately her quivering, lusting body betrays her. She's determined to hide – or at least deny – any attraction to this overly macho male.

Josh turns her over to cradle in his arms declaring,

"The cuddling afterwards is just as important as the spanking."

He leans in to kiss the tears from her face and when his mouth finds her lips she responds with warmth and passion before remembering to be offended.

"That hurt!" she whines with a pout.

"It's supposed to hurt a bit sweetie, that's how your bum becomes such a pretty color, and it makes you squirm and squeal which really turns me on. The dominant male in me loves to have you under my control, in my power, and..." once again Josh strokes between her legs to play with the wet evidence of her arousal before continuing: "the submissive woman in you enjoys getting her bottom warmed."

"I did NOT enjoy that, and I'm not submissive!"

With one hand he toys with her clit while the other is exploring her breasts and teasing her nipples. She arches her back with pleasure and he murmurs in her ear:

"Are you my good girl?" and chuckles when she gasps *Yes!* Before correcting herself to say *no, No, NO!*

"So you say, but it's obvious that my discipline turns you on."

"No it doesn't, I was like this already," she claims.

"You were horny before I got here?" he chuckles, delighted at her stubborn lie.

"If you must know I was masturbating, with my toy. I don't need a man, I have a battery-operated boyfriend. I was outside perfectly relaxed in the privacy of my fenced yard when you came hammering on my door."

"I see. So this," he fingers her again, "is the aftermath of your self-induced orgasm, hmm? Because if so," his fingers move faster and her hips swivel to push her clit forward, "you didn't do a very good job." His voice has dropped to a rumbling vibration in her ear.

"You interrupted me!" she exclaims.

"Then it's only right that I fix things up and finish it for you."

Now he slips his middle finger in her hole while his index finger holds back her labia and her unprotected clit is expertly stroked by his thumb.

"I don't want you to," She's still trying to defy him but her hips are gyrating and the words come out in a pant.

He rubs a wet finger over her lips, making her taste herself, and says:

"Liar."

Ms Conklin is deeply confused and thinks she might start crying again. She's filled with self-loathing for her wanton craving, but equally desirous that this skilful manhandling continue. She doesn't even know this man! She's embarrassed and ashamed of herself but... horribly, that's part of the attraction!

"What's your first name Ms Conklin?"

She refuses to answer and he rubs harder and faster until she cries out *Lucy* as she orgasms.

Holding Lucy tightly in his arms Josh marvels at how soft and warm and silky she is. He's just met this young woman and already he's enslaved by her charms.

"You're absolutely perfect."

"I'm not, my agent is always complaining that I'm too short, my breasts are too big, I have a belly, my butt is too fat, and my legs aren't long enough, and my lips aren't full enough—"

Josh interrupts saying: "You fit perfectly on my lap – face up *or* face down – your breasts are magnificent, my hands love the flare from your waist to your hips, your butt is luscious, your legs are shapely, your lips are delicate... you have a body built to nurture. And a perfect body to play with like this..."

He lays her down on the couch with a pretend growl as he roughly gropes and fondles. His hands quickly travel all over her body, clutching soft flesh, being greedy and grabby. She struggles against his fast-moving fingers but finds herself tickled and pinched, poked and stroked until her nipples are hard, she's giggling and gasping for breath, and the moistness of her arousal has become a pool of sticky slick. She's surprised at how quickly she orgasms again.

Now Josh's mouth is moving as rapidly as his hands and she's being kissed and nipped, suckled, licked and nibbled. When his mouth attaches to her hard nub the third orgasm hits hardest and lasts longest. Her hips buck and her legs tremble.

Now when he asks: "Are you my good girl?"

Lucy looks him right in the eye to answer: "No! I'm your bad girl and you need to fuck me hard!"

He lets out a loud laugh while the two of them spare a moment to revel in their mutual lust. Then Josh quickly strips off his jeans and is soon burying his cock deeply inside Lucy with powerful strokes. Her body welcomes every thrust. She pulls off his t-shirt and pulls him down to feel his skin on hers but he pulls back growling *No, I want to see you* and after watching her breasts bounce to match his rhythm he gazes into her eyes as they cum together.

Lucy is utterly drained. She falls back limply while Josh squeezes her in a very tight hug. Neither one of them understands this instant animal attraction they feel but neither do they encourage any need to question it. It is what it is. They're simply two unattached, healthy and fit young people who induce raging hormones in each other.

Josh rolls onto his back pulling Lucy on top of him. She curls against his chest, listening to his heartbeat while he strokes her blonde curls.

"I know nothing about you," she says.

"I'm 32 so that's what, about 10 years older than you? I'm a bachelor with no kids. I own a Fitness Health Spa that includes a gym, pool, sauna, and because of that I'm putting a stop to this sunbathing of yours. The sun is the absolute worse thing for your skin, you need to wear tons of sunblock outdoors or you run the very real risk of getting skin cancer."

"Well I sunbathe in the nude for my job. I'm a swimsuit model and I can't have any tan lines but I do need my skin to have a healthy color so I will continue to sunbathe – in the nude - and you can't tell me what to do."

His hands grip her backside to remind her that he's already shown what he can do to persuade her. She wriggles her sore bottom but he holds firm.

"Is that why you don't have any hair on your pussy? Because of your modeling?"

Yeah, the bikinis sometimes show about some skin here so I've got to be perfectly smooth and bare. Why, don't you like me hairless?"

"No, I don't. It makes you look too young, I mean I know you're not, you're like twenty-one or twenty-two?"

"I'm twenty-six, but thank you!"

"I like that you're closer to my age even if you look younger," Josh pauses to study Lucy's mound, running his hand up and over it. It certainly is very soft and smooth.

"Well?"

"I like being able to see your shiny red clit so easily, and your skin does feel nice, but couldn't you have some hair?"

Lucy looks down at herself as well agreeing that she could leave a narrow strip of hair right down the middle.

"And in case you're wondering I am a natural blonde," she adds.

"You know, I really don't like the idea of you being a swimsuit model. I hate to think of all those boys and young men jerking off to your magazine photos. I mean, if you're modeling thong swimsuits they'll be cumming all over pictures of your ass. Maybe I should stripe it with a belt so the photographers don't want to use it anymore?"

"It feels like most of the photographers I work with hate women so I'm sure they'd love to see me with a red-hot behind. But Josh, teenage boys don't read magazines like Vogue or Elle and that's where my swimwear and lingerie shots are published."

"Really? Those are major magazines."

"Yes, I make a lot of money. I only do *clean and wholesome* shoots. Well, the Vogue shots can get *artistic* but because it's Vogue that's acceptable. It's all extremely profitable because this kind of work just keeps on coming whereas the skin mags – even top-of-the-line – always want a new face and a new body. Semi-nude shots for Victoria's Secret are always tastefully done too, but they prefer their models to be exclusive."

"Well, you'll just have to be the model with the whitest skin ever. No more nude sunbathing, in fact no more sunbathing at all."

"We'll just see what my agent has to say about that!"

"Remind your agent that if you don't get skin cancer you will get wrinkles. Tell her – or him – to market you as the snow queen or ghostly girl or something."

"Hey, that's pretty good."

"I spend a lot of time marketing my own business."

Lucy lifts herself up to straddle Josh while she talks saying: "Josh, this between us just now, the sex, has been great, really great! But I'm not your business. I'm in charge of my own life, thank you very much."

"No Lucy, not any more. Now that I've found you – and yes, I realize it's only been like an hour or so – I'm head-over-heels crazy about you. I'm not letting you go, you're mine, baby girl."

Her body trembles at his words and that scares her, she's fought her for her independence and isn't willing to give it up because of one fantastic fuck. It's only lust at first sight, right? She's read about *instalust* in her romance novels.

She tries to stand up but he pulls her right back down and traps her feet under his legs. Reaching up he fills each hand with a breast and massages till her nipples poke hard against his palms. Her traitorous nipples send a *zing!* across all her erogenous zones.

Unawares, she begins rocking her pelvis so her clit is once again rubbing Josh's re-awakening cock. He holds her hips steady while he rubs the length of his dick along her slit, getting harder and harder in the juice of their cum, teasingly keeping her clit out of reach. She pushes herself forward but he's far too strong for her to budge him and he withholds her pleasure until she's whimpering.

To her dismay Lucy discovers the act of begging and submitting makes her really horny. She's never, ever been turned on by dominant males - just the opposite, in fact! But Josh has woken something inside that she's never encountered before and now she has to acknowledge her wanton desire to be controlled by him. At least for this moment in time.

He easily shifts her into a new position, belly down while his body hovers over her like a cage, hemming her in and blocking every move she tries to make. He has her well and truly trapped.

She can feel his eyes roving over her and when his deep voice rumbles in her ear the vibration goes right through her body.

"Are you my baby girl?"

"No," she replies and he can hear that she's pouting.

Having her body restrained by his should be making her furiously angry but instead she just wants him to take as much from her as he can, as much as he needs and wants. She never dreamed she could ever think or feel this way.

"That's gotta be the sexiest *No* I've ever heard! You *are* my baby girl, aren't you?"

"No, I'm not! Aaahhhh—-"

Lucy's contradiction is cut short when Josh suddenly pinches her neglected, aching clit. Her hips raise up of their own accord opening and exposing her pussy for entry.

He gives a warm chuckle and pushing her back down replies:

"Not yet, baby girl. I'm still admiring the job I did on your ass. It's such a pretty color, and you sure did wiggle nicely for me."

Filled with shame and angry at him and herself Lucy fights to throw Josh off but her efforts are in vain. He's just too strong.

When she manages to half-twist her upper body enough to look into his face she sees that he's grinning. He finds her struggles amusing and endearing. He loves his mastery of her and quickly bends forward to give her a kiss. Lucy turns away indignantly.

If Josh was still twenty he'd have caved in to his lust long before now but he's spent years disciplining his body with ever-more challenging fitness routines and now can exert iron control. He holds back his own desire while enjoying the mess he's making of Lucy with this torment.

She twists and gyrates, cries and pleads, gasps and groans.

"Are you still going to sunbathe nude?"

"I have to! I really do, but I will talk to my agent on Monday."

"Well you can't sunbathe nude here anyhow, there's been a complaint so that's that."

"Huh! No it's not. There's a fence around my yard, and it's a high one, so if anyone is going to go to the trouble to actually see over it that's their problem, I'll do what I want!"

Joel suddenly releases Lucy but only to upend her across his knee again. Her bottom is still a deep pink from the first spanking but now he's administering much harder strokes across every inch turning her skin rosy red.

Lucy shrieks and fights but Josh has a firm hold and a determined will. He's certain Lucy's delectable behind is going to be kept red-hot for quite some time before she learns her proper place as his well-spanked and well-loved baby girl. At least he hopes so! This is such a pleasurable exercise.

He ignores her threats and her pleas and just keeps smacking her in a steady measured way knowing her bottom can take a lot more punishment.

She quickly realizes he's serious about giving her a thorough going-over and as her flesh burns with each stinging swat her need to capitulate to his wants brings a different kind of heat internally.

In a last-ditch effort to battle against him she kicks her legs in a frenzy. He hooks an ankle around both of hers to secure her firmly and increases the tempo of the paddling.

"You like doing this!" she cries in accusation.

"You're right, I do enjoy this Lucy. I love being dominant and seeing you wiggle your gorgeous ass, feeling how wet you are, hearing you promise to be my good girl. It's all a huge turn-on."

The disciplining continues with Josh's swats moving back and forth from one flushed cheek to the next until Lucy is sobbing, compliant, and so aroused her slick is running down her thighs. She was already on the verge of climax when Josh started spanking her bottom so now, when he massages her burning behind, she can't help but groan loudly with desire. It's so embarrassing!

He moves her to kneel on the couch while he enters her soaking wet pussy from behind and grips her breasts with one hand and manipulates her slippery clit with the other.

His cock feels the exquisite throbbing of her insides pulsing hotly along his entire length. Looking down he enjoys the sight of her bright red bottom as he watches his cock slide in and out while she gasps with pleasure. The heat of her backside against his groin drives him harder and deeper.

Josh pounds her into yet another orgasm then pulls out and shoves his cock in Lucy's mouth, she opens wide to receive him. *She's so willing she must be just as turned on as I am,* he thinks happily.

He's certain he's found his soul-mate, and is delighted to claim her. He tells her he'll mark her bottom again and again until she accepts that she's his.

Lucy foresees a future with many sessions across her man's knee while she disputes his authority over her, despite being equally sure she belongs with him. Belongs *to* him.

She loves this playtime, loves being forced to suck his cock *or else.* Of course the threat of a spanking doesn't necessarily mean she *has* to greedily suck like a nasty slut... but she does anyhow. It's lovely to blame all her naughty urges on his manly domination.

Now she's the one to pull away. Sliding down she spreads her legs and her cunt is a delightful invitation to his aching dick. Lifting her ankles onto his shoulders he bends her legs right back as he plunges into her.

Rapidly and repeatedly squeezing her pussy she pulls him over the edge into ecstasy while pumping every drop of cum out till he's fully drained, enjoying her female power.

"I can dehydrate you any time I want!" she states triumphantly.

Josh pulls her tight against his chest and kisses his way up her throat to her ear where he whispers in his deep voice:

"And I will spank your gorgeous ass and fuck your hungry cunt any time *I* want. In fact, I'm just going to leave my cock here inside you, enjoying the warm wetness."

Lucy snuggles into his embrace with deep satisfaction. She got far more than she expected when she answered the pounding on her front door - and she's just thrilled to have it all.

"Oh Derek, this story plays right into a long-time fantasy of mine except it was Cop and Nude Sunbather. It will be a lot of fun! I'll greet you at the door with nothing except a skimpy towel and while I'm trying to cover myself you'll be pushing your way in with your eyes running all over my body. That will be so hot!"

"I was inspired by how much I enjoy putting you across my knee and spanking your luscious derriere rosy red..."

"Oh, and I love how all of my squirming and wiggling in your lap makes both of us super horny for steaming-hot sex!"

"And sweetheart, I love you."

"I can't wait. Seriously, let's go to bed now and start rehearsing!"

Don't miss out!

Visit the website below and you can sign up to receive emails whenever Lucy Lafferty publishes a new book. There's no charge and no obligation.

https://books2read.com/r/B-A-PTVEC-NNZYC

BOOKS 2 READ

Connecting independent readers to independent writers.

Also by Lucy Lafferty

Santa's Christmas Party with the Littles: a DD/lg Age Play and Age Gap Short Story
A New Year's Resolution for Boss Daddy's Tardy Middle
A Valentine's Day Punishment for a Naughty Middle's Vandalism
Doll Learns a Different Lesson at the St Patrick's Day Masquerade
Dared to Bare
Easter Eggs For Sylvie
Tammy's April Fool's Prank
Celebrating the Fourth of July at Bandits BDSM Club

Watch for more at https://lori-laidlaw-novelist-bvwonn.mailerpage.io/projects-copy.

www.ingramcontent.com/pod-product-compliance
Lightning Source LLC
Chambersburg PA
CBHW020140180626
46810CB00004B/1662